CHASE DEVEREAUX

BERNADETTE MARIE

5 PRINCE PUBLISHING

Published by 5 PRINCE PUBLISHING & BOOKS, LLC

PO Box 865, Arvada, CO 80001

www.5PrinceBooks.com

ISBN digital: 978-1-63112-254-5

ISBN print: 978-1-63112-255-2

Cover Credit: Marianne Nowicki

To Stan,
You were once that guy I referred to as "Only my friend," but I quickly got over that. I love you beyond words. And I'm proud of the life we've made.

ACKNOWLEDGMENTS

To My Men: I see you make those grown up decisions every day, and I'm so proud of each of you. But then you get with your brothers, and you're little kids again. Never lose that!

Mom and Sissy: I love writing these tight knit families because I have so many amazing emotions to draw from. They argue more than we ever did, but we're weird that way.

Cate: I shall forever sing your praises for making me look good. I wish I could always offer you the next book the next day.

To My Book Bees, Street Team, and Readers: Your love of 'friends to lovers' keeps me motivated to bring you the very best stories I can. This is one of my favorite tropes, so I shall always have a new story for you.

CHASE DEVEREAUX

CHAPTER 1

Sun. Why in the hell did it have to be so bright?

Chase lifted his arm and draped it over his face to shield his eyes. The only responsibility he had today was to take the Cadillac limo to pick up his sister and her husband and take them to the airport. He wouldn't have to leave until seven o'clock that night. With the sun blinding him, he knew it was much too early to be up.

He'd tied one on the night before at his sister's wedding. What did they expect? They'd had it at the tap house her husband owned. Of course, had he stuck to beer, he might have been okay. But they'd brought in other liquor since it was a private event, and he'd taken part in it. Boy had he.

There were some fuzzy spots in his memory when he thought about the night. One thing was for certain, he knew he hadn't driven home, but he wasn't sure how he got home.

Lifting his arm from his face, he opened one eye and looked around. Yep, this was his house, and his horribly decorated bedroom.

That smelly dog bed still sat in the corner, and that poor, old hound dog had crossed the rainbow bridge months ago. God, he missed that dog.

As he lowered his arm, someone turned in the bed next to him. Their arm came over his chest and he froze. It wasn't the first time he'd had a woman in his bed that he hadn't remembered bringing there. There were some unfortunate effects of alcohol. Sometimes he didn't remember bringing anyone home with him. Other times, he'd bring them home and not be able to perform and they'd both just pass out. There wasn't any pride in it, but then, he didn't feel guilty either.

He picked up the hand that rested on his chest and examined it. At least there wasn't a ring on the finger. He'd been known to find that from time to time. Though Chase liked to have fun, and a willing woman was just his cup of joe, he did believe in the sanctity of marriage for those who had ventured into it. Sleeping with someone's wife wasn't his thing.

Auburn hair splayed out over the pillow next to him, and the woman's face was turned the other direction.

But as she moved ever so slightly again, he saw the tell-tale sign and he knew exactly who he'd taken to bed with him.

Only one woman he knew of had a butterfly tattoo in watercolor on her left shoulder blade. He would always remember it because he'd gone with her when she'd gotten it. And somehow, she'd convinced him to get the same tattoo in the same place.

Over the years he'd convinced others that it was in memory of his grandmother who had passed when he was little. But that was just bullshit so no one would think he was some kind of sissy with a butterfly tattoo.

When she turned her head to the side and faced him, Chase watched as she opened her eyes—those emerald green eyes. At least she smiled next and didn't come up swinging.

She let out a sigh. "Well, crap. We ended up here again, didn't we?" Her voice was raspy from sleep.

"Looks like it."

"We're never going to hear the end of this."

"My sister leaves for her honeymoon in a few hours. If she saw us leave together, she'll have forgotten about it by the time she gets back."

"Then again, if she saw us, she would have stopped us."

That was true, he thought.

Hillary Mills rolled onto her back and pulled the sheet up to cover herself. Hillary, his sister's best friend and employee, had been in his bed more than this one time. A one-night stand years ago had stirred up enough trouble for them. They'd promised they'd never do it again, as it seemed to have upset his sister Kennedy quite a bit.

More than likely it was the looseness of morals surrounding the idea of a one-night stand that bothered Kennedy, and to think it had happened between her brother and best friend had been inconceivable for her. But that kind of crap happened all the time to Chase.

He knew the side of Hillary that was a party girl. And she knew his side. So as long as they didn't make this awkward, they could enjoy what had happened—as soon as they remembered it.

Hillary took his hand and interlaced their fingers, which he thought was a bit intimate. "When did you get the sporty car?" she asked.

"Is that what we drove home in?"

"Yep."

"I don't own a sporty car. You stole someone's ride, Hill."

She laughed that throaty laugh that always twisted him up inside. "Well, shit. I guess we're going to jail. You know what they do to sexy boys like you, don't you?"

Chase swallowed hard. Why was she being playful and intimate? Wasn't she freaked out by this too?

"I'm glad you think I'm sexy, but I don't even want to think about what they do to guys like me."

She laughed again and he had to close his eyes and will away the feelings that it stirred in him.

"I'm starving. What do you have to eat here?"

He gave it some thought. "Frozen burritos."

"Gross."

"That's what I have."

"Let's get dressed and go get breakfast. My treat."

Chase rubbed his eyes. "What time is it?"

Hillary rolled over, the sheets adjusting to give him a full view of her. "It's three o'clock in the afternoon."

"There's that burger place at the end of the block," he offered.

"Yeah, I could go for that."

They laid there a moment longer, as if neither of them were willing to stand up and expose themselves to the other one.

Finally, Hillary sat up on the edge of the bed. "Do you have something I can wear? I'm not putting on that dress again."

Chase looked across the room at the pink bridesmaid dress draped over a chair. "I don't know what would freak my sister out more; us in here naked together, or that dress in that condition."

"It's a toss-up."

"There are T-shirts in the closet, and I have some sweatpants in the drawer."

"This many clothes on the floor and you still have clothes put away?"

He wanted to make some stupid comment about keeping clean clothes put away for the women who need them, but he thought better of it. This was Hillary after all. She deserved more respect.

"Consider me only half a slob."

She stood and walked to the closet. Everything about her made everything about him react all at once.

Hillary pulled a shirt from a hanger and slid it over her body, pulling her hair out from under the collar and letting it cascade down her back. "I don't think you're a slob. Maybe it makes you the creative lover that you are," she complimented as she bent over to take a pair of sweatpants out of the drawer.

It was a shame that out of respect for his sister, there would never be anything between him and Hillary, because if she thought he was creative when he was drunk, she'd really appreciate him when he was sober.

CHAPTER 2

Hillary excused herself to wander down the hall to the bathroom, where Chase's towels lay in a pile on the floor. With any other man she would be disgusted, but for some reason she found it adorable. And, because she was her, she picked up the towels and hung them on the rack like a normal human would.

She looked in the mirror and faced the facts of what she'd done. Her eyes were black from makeup. Her hair wore the badge of too much hairspray and all of the pins missing from the updo that had taken an hour to anchor in.

Standing in Chase Devereaux's bathroom, looking like she did right now, was something she'd promised herself to never do again. One time, a long time ago, was supposed to be it. Now here she was, tangled up with him again, and with Chase, it only lasted one night. And that was a shame, because completely drunk, he was sensitive and mindful to her.

She deserved this, she supposed. Though she'd never have let on, she'd been insanely jealous of Kennedy's relationship with Joel. Four men start working on a business next door, one is married, two don't show any interest, and Kennedy gets the other one. And wouldn't you know it, that ended in marriage with a baby in the carriage.

Hillary turned on the water in the sink and let it warm as she took one last look at her pathetic face. This was a walk of shame if she'd ever seen one. Last one, she promised herself. Maybe it was time to own up to being a grown up and stop having walk of shame mornings. It was time to find a man who was interested in a relationship that lasted more than twelve hours.

There was some kind of solace in the fact that Chase had mentioned going out into public with her for food. They were friends. They'd been friends a long time, so of course he would take care of her differently than any other woman. But she couldn't get caught up in that or read anything into it.

When the water was warm, she splashed her face with it, and rubbed the dark circles from her eyes, only to expose a different layer of dark circles, caused by too much alcohol and lack of sleep. Studying herself in the mirror, dressed in Chase's T-shirt, she thought of the million things she had to do today, including cleaning Kennedy's store before opening on Monday. But all she wanted to do was get some food, go home and sleep this off.

"You are the most freaking beautiful woman I have ever known. Do you know that?" Chase's voice grumbled from the doorway.

His hair was disheveled, and his face shadowed by the darkness of whiskers that had had a day's worth of growth. He was an Adonis in a pair of loose boxers.

"That's quite a trophy to have," she admitted as she turned to use his towel to dry her face. "I know the competition is steep when it comes to beautiful women and Chase Devereaux."

Was there a flash of regret in his eye before he turned up the corner of his mouth into that sexy smile, she wondered.

"You're different. I would have thought you knew that."

That landed a hard blow in her stomach, and she pressed her hand to it to keep it from flopping again.

"Why am I different?" she asked with a need to hear the answer.

Chase stepped in and pulled her to him, pressing a kiss to her neck which left her knees wobbly. "You've always been different. I care about you more than I've ever cared about any other woman."

Her hands came to his firm shoulders to steady herself. This was what would land her in his bed again. She couldn't do that.

"Because I'm Kennedy's friend?"

"Yes." He tucked a strand of her hair behind her ear. "And my friend. You didn't find out about my family and think I was some bastard child who didn't deserve a friend."

"Your story is unique and not your fault."

He nodded. "Makes for a messed up childhood though. Brothers and sisters everywhere, and your parents don't belong together at all."

Hillary let herself sink in closer to him, running her hand down his back. When Kennedy was born, her father had had an affair with Chase's mom, and then Chase was born. His father had gone back to Kennedy's mom and had one more son. He'd stepped up and been a participating father, that much Hillary knew. But it had destroyed two families.

Chase's mother went on to marry another man and have more children and his father married again and their sister Paige was born. But he was right, it was like being an only child stuck in the middle of different families.

Her cheek brushed against the whiskers on his jaw and her knees wobbled. She was a sucker for him, and she knew she was about to take another turn in the bed that next week another woman would occupy. Hillary owed herself more than this. Where was her respect for herself? Where was her respect for him? Where was her control when it came to Chase Devereaux?

His lips grazed her collarbone and he had to know that did her in, because she became his again in that moment.

Chase's hands made quick work to release her from the T-shirt and sweatpants that she'd borrowed, and he even managed to reach around her and turn on the shower.

When she pulled back to see what he was doing, those blue eyes seared into her and that smile of his melted her into a puddle of goo. When would she ever stop looking and him and wondering what they could have together if they were different people? This was for today, that was all that was promised, but suddenly Hillary wanted more. She wanted a life like Kennedy had just stepped into, but her jealousy over it would have to be worked on because happily ever after just wasn't for people like her and Chase.

Chase kicked off his boxers and turned her to face the shower. She stepped over the side of the tub and he joined her, pulling the curtain closed. Tipping her head back, she let the water drench her hair, and it allowed Chase access to her neck again.

One more time, she thought as he pressed himself to her.

One more time and then she would only pursue that happily ever after, and she knew it meant leaving any feelings she had for Chase behind.

CHAPTER 3

Hillary wasn't sure how she'd managed to keep Chase's company after they'd eaten. But he'd agreed to go to Kennedy's store and help her clean. It never took long. Kennedy kept the store in immaculate condition.

It only took an hour to dust the shelves, vacuum the carpets, clean the bathroom, and restock the beverages.

The tap house next door was back to business as usual. Any remnants of the wedding from the night before had been whisked away with the rental truck.

Chase moved in behind her, wrapping his arms around Hillary's waist as she stood at the break room window drying the glasses they'd celebrated with the day before.

"Why is it I can't keep my hands off you when you're this close to me and we're alone?"

Hillary closed her eyes tight as he kissed the back of her neck. Promises to herself were never kept.

"Chase."

He moaned against her neck.

"Maybe you should go get things situated for Kennedy and Joel. You have to pick them up soon."

He moved her hair to the side and kept working his lips on her neck. "Seven. I have to pick them up at seven. Seven," he repeated, and she knew it wasn't for her that he'd repeated it. Kennedy would lose it if he were late. In fact, Hillary would bet that there were alarms set on his phone that he didn't even know about.

For her own good, she turned to face him and eased him back. Her heart was already breaking, knowing that this attention he was spilling on her was short lived.

"Really. Maybe you should go."

Chase eased back but kept his eyes on her. "What's wrong?"

"Nothing. I just have things to do."

His finger came to her chin and lifted her eyes to meet his. "Seriously, what's wrong?"

"You and I can't act like this is normal. It's not."

He chuckled. "It is normal."

This time she took a step back from him and then another. "No. This happened one time and it hurt Kennedy. Now it happened again, and it's going to hurt her again."

"Screw Kennedy. She's a grown woman with a husband and apparently a baby on the way. She can handle this."

"What is this exactly? We got drunk at their wedding and I made sure you got home. We did it again."

He moved to her, but when she flinched, he stepped back. "And if you weren't freaking out, we could be doing it again."

"Right. For how long? Today? Then you'll go pick them up and I'll come to work tomorrow and that'll be it. We'll see each other in passing like we do, but sometime this week you'll drive a bachelorette party around and go home with one of the bridesmaids."

CHASE TOOK a step back and ran his hand over the growth on his chin. She was right.

He'd never had feelings for any other woman—only for Hillary. But the only other time he'd managed to get her into his bed, things fell apart. If they kept this up, their whole friendship might dissolve, and he couldn't afford for that to happen.

He blew out a breath and dragged his fingers through his hair. "I guess that's that, huh?"

"I guess so."

"This sucks."

"It does," she agreed as she moved back to the glasses she'd been drying and set them up on the shelf.

Chase paced a few circles in the break room of his sister's store. Maybe they could change things. Right here. Right now.

"Are you sure, because I love you, and you know that."

Hillary chuckled. "I love you too, and isn't that our problem? We have too much respect for each other? How long have we been friends, and we've done this twice? Once was too much. Twice was too many."

Women often twisted him up inside. He'd gotten used to it. But this one, hell, she'd been messing with his mind since he was a teenager. Not that she was a tease or anything of the sort, but when he said he loved her, he meant it.

He moved to her and pulled her into his arms. This time her hands came to his shoulders, and she pressed her forehead to his.

"I'll always have that sissy tattoo to remind me of our time together," he chuckled, and she did the same.

"It's a beautiful sentiment."

"On a man it's out of place."

"You're right there. Consider it a reminder of the time we've had together. A memory of me, the one you really love," she teased. She didn't know it was breaking his heart, but he figured it was all the better this way. If they tried to make something of this, he'd end up breaking her heart.

"I love you, Hillary. I'm always here for you."

"And I love you, and ditto." She kissed the tip of his nose, and he knew at that moment whatever they'd had was over.

"Your car is out back, right? And you have your keys?" he asked.

"I'm all set," she said, leaning a hip against the counter. "You're good?"

"I'm good," he said, backing toward the door. "I'll pick my sister up at seven and take her to the airport."

"She'll appreciate that."

He wasn't ready to walk out the door. "I'm going to help the guys out next door while Joel is gone. I'm serving tomorrow and I think they have a taco truck on the schedule to be outside. Maybe you can stop by after work."

Hillary nodded. "That does sound good. Paige is working with me here tomorrow, and I guess with you at the tap house afterwards. She wants to buy a yoga studio?"

"That's what she says. Max is going to stop by after work too. We could have a big family gathering," he said and then felt the queasiness of his statement swirl in his belly. And wasn't that what was wrong here? Hillary was family. He'd just said it.

"I'll be there then. Give Kennedy and Joel my best. I'll talk to you tomorrow."

And that was it, his final dismissal. He contemplated one more kiss, but he thought better of it and held up a hand in a wave instead.

When he let himself out of his sister's store, he stood on the street for just a moment to gather himself. This hurt a hell of a lot more than it should have. When had he actually fallen in love with Hillary?

CHAPTER 4

C hase pulled the limo up to Joel's house and sat for a moment. He'd arranged the back specifically for his sister. The lighting was done in hues of pink, there was non-alcoholic champagne, which he'd had to buy special, on his way to pick her up, after her announcement at the altar that she was pregnant.

They were headed to Paris for one of the fashion shows she attended every year, but this year it had become a honeymoon.

He was happy for her. The Devereauxs weren't quick to find love. They were all a little gun shy because their father scattered it around so much. Except for Paige, he thought. Their dad and her mom had truly been in love. Paige was born from absolute love and it showed in the compassion she could give to others. Max felt jilted because he felt as if he were the child born out of spite when their father went back to their mother. It was a freaking mess. That's all it was.

Chase stepped out of the car and adjusted his jacket. He'd worn his full uniform to give his sister the full effect of the ride. She deserved the best. No one but Kennedy could have kept them all together like she had over the years. Now she was married and expecting a baby. Things surely had changed, and he was happy for that. But still in the back of his mind were thoughts of Hillary and how he'd wished he could have changed his sister's mind on his involvement with Hillary.

Chase walked to the front door and rang the doorbell.

When his sister answered the door, he could have sworn she glowed. She couldn't have been more than a few weeks pregnant, but it had already changed her.

"You look snazzy," she said as she opened the door for him to step inside.

"Only the best for you."

"Joel is getting our last bag," she said as she reached for her suitcase.

Chase moved faster and reached it. "Full service, ma'am. I've got this."

He took the suitcase out to the car and gently slid it into the trunk. A moment later Joel carried the other bag out to him.

"This is really nice of you to drive us to the airport and to cover for a few weeks. I owe you one."

"No problem. Anything for her," he said nodding toward his sister.

"I don't think she knows Hillary took you home last night. Is that off the table for conversation? I don't want to dredge up something and get in trouble on my honeymoon."

Chase shook his head. "It's off the table. She wasn't a fan the first time we hooked up. Best not let her know she stayed with me all night."

A tight grin formed on Joel's lips, and Chase knew he understood the situation. And because he'd come to understand the man that Joel was, he knew his sister would never be the wiser.

Kennedy hurried down the front steps as Chase moved to the side of the car and opened the door. "Paris awaits, ma'am."

"Thank you, sir," she said playing along.

~

WHEN CHASE RETURNED HOME from the airport, he hung his uniform up in the closet. Nothing else in his life might be in order, but the uniform and anything having to do with his business was kept neat and tidy.

His first limousine was a fluke buy. Someone had a deal on one, and he thought it would be funny to call that his car. Then he picked up a few fairs and realized that the money making potential was there. It came in handy after he got laid off from his job, and started to make money with it. Before he knew it, he needed another limo and another driver—then two more drivers. Now he had three limos, a staff of drivers, and a coveted client list. His business was the only thing that ran smoothly in his life, because he had so much pride in it.

As he looked around the small house, he realized he'd only been coming and going for years. This wasn't the home of someone who lived at all. It was a glorified hotel room without room service or maid service.

Chase slipped into a pair of shorts and a tank, even though it was arctic outside, he was plenty warm inside. He picked up all of the paper plates that were scattered in the living room, most of them with pizza crust still on them, and threw them in the trash. He reran the dishwasher, and then added the dishes that cluttered the sink when that load had finished.

He swapped out the towels in the bathroom for clean ones and threw the others in the laundry. Clean towels made the bathroom look even dirtier, so he made quick work of it next and in no time it sparkled.

Then he walked into his room. How was it he could get women into that bed at all? Clothes covered the floor and the bedding was falling off. Well, that was a testament to the night he'd had with Hillary.

And then his heart ached. She deserved more than a one-night stand. She deserved the whole package, and he wasn't the guy to give that to her.

Wasn't it sad, he'd been away from her for a few hours and he missed her desperately.

Pulling the sheets off the bed, he piled them with the clothes that he'd picked up off the floor. His mother made sure he had plenty of sheets, so clean ones were always available. Perhaps he should change them more often, he thought as he began to make up the bed.

The nightstands were cleared of their snack containers and empty glasses. The recycle container was filled with empty beer bottles, and the trash can, well it should have been much fuller than it was. He took back the half slob comment. He was a full-on slob.

But what he noticed as the room began to look better was there were no condoms or condom wrappers. That wasn't like him at all. No matter what the woman said to him, he used protection. Though growing up, not getting a girl pregnant was hammered into his head, the thought of catching something worried him more.

Had he had this conversation with Hillary? He couldn't even remember the creative sex she'd said they had; how could he have been coherent enough to think about asking her if she was covered. Oh, he was an idiot. He'd seduced her into the shower too, and there certainly was no condom used there.

Hillary was a smart woman. Of course, she was covered—and she'd dismissed him. So, he wasn't going to worry about it. He gathered the rest of the trash and continued to better his lifestyle by cleaning his home.

CHAPTER 5

Hillary looked down at her freshly painted fingernails. *Kennedy Pink* shimmered back at her.

Kennedy had thought of everything when she left Hillary in charge while she was in Paris. Even making sure that the weekly manicure she had scheduled was given to Hillary, and Kennedy had covered the bill on that.

Hillary pushed open the signature pink doors to Kennedy's store and walked inside. Everything about the store was feminine, right down to the smell.

The jewelry that Kennedy designed sparkled in the morning light. The chandeliers twinkled as the sunlight hit them through higher windows. When Kennedy had set up her dream store, she knew what she was doing.

The door opened behind her, and Hillary turned to see Kennedy's younger sister Paige walk in with a Starbucks drink in each hand.

"After this weekend, we need sugar and caffeine," she joked and Hillary knew that if the vegan Paige was filling her body with bad things, she must need a pick me up.

She took the drink that was handed to her and took a sip. "Sinful."

"Seriously," Paige agreed as she took a long sip with her eyes closed. "I feel as if there should be a sort of confession when I do this."

"It's between you and your maker, right?"

"Amen to that. But I'm going to need a gallon of water just to wash this out of my system. When you don't eat sugar, and then you indulge in wedding cake and sugary coffee drinks, you pay for it, and you pay large."

Paige set her drink on the counter and took her bag to Kennedy's office where she stored it before walking back out to the showroom. "Do we have a lot of shipments today?"

Hillary shook her head. "No. Since she's in Paris, she didn't buy as much, but when she gets home, I'll be labeling things until my hands bleed."

"Good. Not about your hands. Just I'm glad it won't be too much today. Seriously, I'm exhausted. I worked the tap house last night, and for a Sunday, it was packed. I'm glad Joel gave me the job. I'm cleaning up on tips."

"Gave you the job? You blackmailed him into it."

"I did," she said proudly as she toasted the air with her drink. "Kennedy is so freaking stubborn she could have messed up a really good thing had I not stepped in and blackmailed him." She smiled and Hillary knew she was proud of getting her way. "I'm closer to my goal of raising half of the money for the yoga studio. I might not have to borrow as much money as I'd thought. But it's kicking my ass."

Hillary had never had a dream to own something, not the way the Devereauxs did. Kennedy had her store. Chase had his limos. Max ran his construction company, and Paige currently taught yoga, but wanted to own her own studio. They were motivated.

"Where is this studio?"

Paige looked around the store as if maybe someone would be there to overhear. "The holistic healing at the end of this building. The woman who owns it is looking to retire. She told those of us who work there first, and I've built a good following for my yoga practice. It would be the best thing for me to stay there and revamp the space."

"But this is under the strictest of confidence, as to the location that is?"

"It is. She's still on the fence, and she doesn't want someone sweeping in and disrupting things. I get it, but I hate secrets."

So did Hillary, and didn't she have a doozy?

She was saved from her wallowing in self-pity when the door opened and Joel's mother walked in.

"Good morning, ladies. I just got a text that said they were boarding their international flight, so they're on their way to Paris."

Paige moved her drink to the lower level of the counter, as Kennedy had long ago trained them to do. "They're going to have a great time. Well she is. When he sits at one of those fashion shows, he might reconsider what he got himself into."

June Kingsley laughed. "He loves her too much to even assume he'll be miserable." She set her purse on the counter. "I'm looking for a pocketbook," she said as she pulled hers from the worn leather purse that she carried. "This one seems to have seen better days."

Paige took it from her and examined it. "You're looking for plenty of space too. We unboxed some really nice ones last week. C'mon, I'll show them to you."

June picked up her purse and followed Paige across the store. Kennedy lucked out in the mother-in-law department, Hillary thought as she took her drink to the office to sort through the emails that Kennedy would usually attend to on Mondays.

~

CHASE PARKED his car in the lot and killed the engine. He'd seen the taco truck setting up, and his stomach was already grumbling at the thought of hot tacos.

He glanced out the window and noticed Hillary's car was still parked at his sister's store. A quick look at his watch and he realized he had a full ten minutes before Jeff was expecting him to be behind the bar. Just enough time to say hello.

The back door was always unlocked, and he let himself inside. Paige sat at the small table dipping a tea bag in and out of the mug of water that sat before her.

"You lost?" she asked as he stepped inside. "Kennedy would kill you for walking in the back door."

"It's Monday. You don't show clothes on Monday, so there are no half-clad women walking around."

She nodded in agreement. "You heading over to the tap room?"

"Yeah. I heard you had a killer night last night."

"The Kingsleys knew what they were doing when they opened here. I guess that's what Olde Town needed."

"Certainly did," he said as he saw Hillary walk into the room, her attention distracted by the pink clipboard in her hands.

"Did you see the box with the..." she stopped mid-sentence when she saw Chase standing in the room. "Oh, hi." Her voice shook when she talked to him, and it did a little something to his heart to hear it.

"Hey."

She blinked a few times and refocused on the chart. "Did you see the box with the opal earrings come in. Three sets?"

"Already marked and on display," Paige acknowledged.

"Thanks." Hillary turned and left the room.

A moment later Paige pulled back and punched Chase right in the arm.

He jumped back and held his hand to the affected area. "What in the hell was that for? Crap."

"What are you doing?"

"I'm standing here watching you drown that stupid tea bag."

"That's not what I'm talking about and you know it," she scolded in a hushed voice. "What's going on between the two of you?"

"Nothing."

"You're lying."

This was a lost cause. He sat down next to her. "We went home together after the wedding. I'd like it if you kept that quiet."

Paige shook her head. "Kennedy is going to be pissed."

"I'm thirty-six-freaking-years-old. I'm not afraid of my sister."

"It's not a matter of fear. It's a matter of respect. Hillary is her best friend. You're her brother. You did this once before and it rocked her world."

He didn't want to hear this. The guilt already was killing him. "I care for her. I really do."

"So, you're an item?"

"She doesn't want that. She's thinking of Kennedy too."

"But you want that?"

All he could do was shrug.

Paige shook her head again and set her face so that she looked like a disappointed mother. "So, it's dropped? We're not saying anything about it to anyone?"

He leaned over and kissed his sister on the cheek. "Exactly. It's between us only."

She nodded, but he hadn't won her over with any of his answers, he knew that.

"I gotta get to work. I love you. I'll see you in a bit. Tacos. Remember."

"I don't eat meat."

"They have veggie ones. What a waste." As he stood, he gave her a playful punch to the shoulder and strained to see into the other room where Hillary sat at the desk in his sister's office. She looked beautiful there, professionally dressed with her legs crossed and her fingers tapping on the keyboard. He'd take that vision to work with him and keep hope that she'd come over when she was done for the day.

CHAPTER 6

Hillary locked the door to the shop just past six and looked at the tap house and the crowd that had amassed on a cold Monday night. No one would miss her if she didn't stop.

The extra stress was unnecessary. She and Chase would be okay in a few weeks. Their night together would be water under the bridge, and they'd have their friendship intact. It was nice to have someone tell her they loved her though. Even if she understood the context in which it had been said.

"You going in?" The voice behind her was as familiar to her as her own, and she turned to see Max Devereaux walking up to her. He leaned forward and kissed her cheek with his cold lips. He was dressed casually, as he usually was in work boots and jeans. His thick coat was zipped up and the collar pulled up to keep his neck warm.

"I was contemplating it. But I think I'll go home."

"You look too nice to just go home. Though I'm going to guess your feet are freezing."

Hillary looked down at her feet. Heels were never a fashion

statement in the snow. "It's a little chilly around here. I'll just head home."

He wrapped his arm around her waist. "Nope. You're my date now. Let's have a beer and a taco. Then you can go home. Neither of us need to be lonely tonight."

"You're still lonely?" she asked taking a jab at him and his sad love life.

"When the woman you love chooses her career over you and moves across the country, you choose to be lonely. It's not worth putting yourself through that again."

"And it doesn't help when you see her on TV every time you flip through the channels," she dug a little deeper.

Max shook his head. "It's a good thing I like you. Besides, I don't pay for those channels. Who wants to cook something from scratch, when there are taco trucks? You're my date?"

How could she refuse the offer? Max Devereaux was as good as they came, and if he was lonely, the world was indeed a sad place.

They walked through the door, Max's arm still around her waist. Immediately she saw Paige sitting at a table with Joel's sister-in-law Dina and her children. Paige waved and Max acknowledged it with a wave of his own.

Max led her to the bar where Chase smiled when he saw her, and then his eyes flickered dark as he noticed Max's arm around her waist. But a moment later his smile was back.

"You made it," he said to her and she smiled up at him.

Max gave her a squeeze. "She's my date tonight. No need to just be lonely at home," he said as he looked up at the menu. "Give me that Gregory Stout. What would you like? It's on me."

Hillary swallowed hard. "I'll take the same one," she said, remembering that it was the beer she and Chase had started on after the wedding.

Without another word, Chase filled the glasses and slid them toward them. "Starting a tab, brother?"

"Yep. Me and my gal will be back for more."

He slid his arm around her waist again, and they headed to join Paige at the table.

As Hillary sat down, she managed one more glance in Chase's direction. His cheeks were red with anger and his eyes were narrowed. Surely, he understood that Max was innocently making a scene. She had no more feelings for Max than anyone else in the bar—anyone but him.

"Did she call?" Paige asked as Hillary settled in and draped her coat over the back of the chair.

"Yes. They had just landed before I closed up. Though I'm sure it wasn't a call to update me on where she was. It was a call to see if we ran the store okay today."

"I figured. But we did okay," Paige said, lifting her gluten-free beer choice in salute.

Hillary did the same and took a long drink from her glass.

CHASE TURNED to distract himself by washing the glasses that had accumulated behind him. Kendra was the busser for the night, and she was on top of making sure the tables were clear. She was new to the tap house and he hadn't had a chance to talk to her much.

He looked back at the table and saw his brother's arm wrap about Hillary's shoulders. What in the hell was going on? She wouldn't give him an opportunity, but Max could just sweep in like that. That was bullshit and he was going to let him know as much.

However, that would have to come later. A party of nice-looking women were standing at the bar looking at the selection of beers.

"Hey, ladies," he greeted them, grinning like he would when he'd want them to drop their phone numbers in the jar. "What are we thinking?"

The blonde with the bobbed haircut tucked her hair behind her ear. "I have never been to a tap room. So, you don't have hard alcohol, and no Budweiser, huh?"

He leaned in, and it caused her to do the same. "Nope. No Bud here." He pushed the menu of beer selections so that it was intimately tucked between them. "We have craft beers from all the local breweries. These are your light ones, and these are more stout." He pointed to the listings.

"What's a flight?"

"We can set you ladies up with a small glass of each of them to try. It's the best way to go if you're new to the craft brewery world."

The blonde in front of him batted long lashes and licked those pouty pink lips. "Let's do that. Do I pay now?"

"Or I can start you a tab."

The brunette next to her nudged her. "Start a tab." She winked at Chase. "We'll stick around a little."

And that was how his nights usually started. He turned to get the rack for the flight and filled the glasses while looking out over the crowd but landing his gaze back on Hillary.

Friends. They were friends. He was supposed to move on.

He set the rack in front of the women who stood wide eyed looking at it. He gave them the rundown of each beer and what to expect. When they turned around, he watched them walk away with appreciation. Yeah, he could move on. Hillary was only one night.

HILLARY DRANK her beer and pushed the glass to the center of the table. She'd been there an hour, and it was an hour longer than she'd planned. Getting home, out of the clothes she'd worn all day, and sliding into a bubble bath were all she could think about.

"I think I'm going to call it a night."

Max quickly finished his beer and picked up both glasses. "I'll walk you to your car."

He stood, shrugged on his coat, and helped her with hers. She gave Paige a hug, told Dina goodnight, and walked out of the bar with Max, just as they'd walked in with his arm around her waist. She'd noticed him motion to Chase that he'd be back in.

Hillary pulled her jacket tighter. "I think the temperature dropped another ten degrees."

"I think it's been a colder winter than usual."

"Are you going back in?"

"I think so. I could use one more beer. It was a rough day."

Hillary pressed the button on her key fob. "I'm sorry to hear that."

"Part of the line of work I'm in. Drive safe, okay? There were some slick spots driving over here."

"I'll be fine."

Max leaned in and pressed a kiss to her cheek, just as he had when he'd first caught up with her. "Good night."

"Good night."

He waited until her car was started and she was driving away from the curb. Max Devereaux, he was certainly different than his brother, and that was charming in its own right. But both the Devereaux men were off limits. Her loyalty was to Kennedy.

CHAPTER 7

C hase watched his brother walk back in the front door without Hillary wrapped in his arm. But had they kissed goodnight?

What the hell would it matter? The blonde had already given him her number, and he had half a mind to call her.

Max walked back to the bar and looked up at the menu.

"Let's try that saison."

"You're an asshole. Do you know that?"

Max turned his attention to his brother, eyes wide. "I beg your pardon?"

"You walk in here with Hillary as if you own the place. Who do you think you are?"

Max blinked and narrowed his gaze on him. "You know what. Just tell me what I owe and I'll get out of your way. You seem to have a stick shoved up your ass and I'm not interested in being part of whatever pity party you're throwing."

"Just go. I'll cover your drinks."

Max shook his head as he pulled his wallet out of his pocket. He threw a twenty on the counter. "Keep the change. Maybe it'll help your attitude."

"Why don't you and I step outside, little brother?"

"Why don't we?"

Max shoved his wallet back into his pocket, walked out the back door and Chase followed.

He watched as Max walked so that they were out of sight of everyone else. When he turned around, Chase pulled back and punched him right across the jaw. He went down with the blow, right into the snowbank, and blood from his lip stained the fresh snow on the ground.

"What in the hell is wrong with you?" Max shouted as he got to his feet and rammed his head into Chase's belly, throwing him back into another snowbank and ending the landing with a punch to the gut.

Chase could see his breath carry in the air as he held his stomach, his brother panting next to him.

Max held his hand to his bleeding lip.

"You're a son-of-a-bitch!" Max shouted, but obviously not fearful for his life, as he sat on the cold ground next to Chase. "What in the hell was that about?"

"Hillary."

"What did I do to her to cause that? I brought her in and bought her a beer. You are a complete asshole if you think that was mistreating her."

The pain his brother had caused him eased as the pang of guilt took over. "Don't make a move on her, man."

"Hillary? She's like a sister. Why would I make a move on her? First of all, Kennedy would kill me. Secondly, I'm not interested in her. She's not my type. She is my friend, and I don't like getting the shit knocked out of me over it. So why don't you mind your own freaking business?"

Max managed to his feet and held out his hand to Chase.

Reluctantly, Chase took it, but he couldn't stand straight yet. He hadn't remembered his brother could land a blow like that.

"Sorry, man," Chase said. "I'm a bit out of sorts."

"I should knock you on your ass again and leave you. Seriously, what is this about?"

Chase managed to walk off the pain as he paced the cold parking lot. "Hillary and I hooked up."

Max took a step toward him and Chase took two back.

"You what? What a douche bag."

He deserved that. "It's not the first time, but it was the last."

"You did that before? And you're still living?"

"Well, it seems you're the only one who didn't know about it. Yeah, Kennedy let me live."

"You're one lucky bastard."

"I am," he said, but he decided it wasn't because Kennedy had given him a pass on what he'd done, but because he'd done it. He was lucky to have those few moments in his memory with Hillary. "We ended up together after the wedding."

"What did Kennedy say about that?"

"She doesn't know. And she's not going to find out."

"Damn straight she's not." Max ran his fingers through his hair. "Unless you and Hillary have feelings?"

And there was the problem. "I think I do, man."

"You're not one to do that."

"I know. I'm not always going to be some scum bag, and I know that's what you're thinking of me. I have feelings."

"And you have them for Hillary?"

"I do."

"Then tell her that."

Chase walked another circle in the snow because the cold was causing the pain in his stomach to amplify. "I did. I even told her I love her."

Max moved in, and Chase moved back again, afraid he'd be on his ass in a second.

"You told her you loved her? What the hell? You don't just fling that around."

"It's Hillary. It wasn't being flung around. Even if it's not all in like Kennedy and Joel, I do love her."

"You're in deep."

There was no denying that now. Hell, he'd punched his brother just for walking into the bar with her.

He pulled Max to him with one arm and pressed a noisy kiss to the top of his head. "God, I'm sorry."

"You should be. You are the biggest asshole I know."

"I am. Let me buy you a beer for busting your lip."

"First, what are you going to do about Hillary?"

Chase wiped his hands over his pants to knock off the dirt. "We agreed it was a mistake, again. We promised it wouldn't happen, again, and we wouldn't even mention it Kennedy. It's too important to dwell on and let it ruin what we have—a solid friendship."

Max shook his head and put his arm around Chase's shoulders. "I don't know if you can just let it be. I have heard you talk about a lot of women. A lot, you whore. But I have never heard you talk about one with the sincerity that you talk about Hillary. Maybe let it lay for a bit. Get your feet under you. But, shit, maybe she got into you deeper than you thought she did."

Chase was sure of that. Nothing made him react the way seeing Max walk in with her had. He was screwed if Hillary actually did move on and he had to watch some other man care for her.

He never would have expected to feel this way about anyone. How was he going to move on from it?

CHAPTER 8

Hillary wiped her hand over the steamed-over mirror in her bathroom and wrapped her hair up in a towel.

She opened the drawer of her cabinet and pulled out the small pocket calendar she kept in there where she marked off the days until Kennedy and Joel returned. She had three more days to run the store, a week to help Kennedy get situated with the inventory and the expected purchases she made, and then Hillary was going to take a week off.

It would be her first vacation in two years. Vacation, as in getting on an airplane, flying to a beach, and sunning herself while she drank margaritas.

She'd been saving for the trip for nearly two years, and she'd thought Kennedy would go with her. Who would have thought some guy would come along and sweep her off her feet.

Besides, it was still cold there in the beginning of March. Mexico was calling her name.

She had heard from Kennedy a few times since they'd been in Paris. The fashion shows were the week earlier, and now they were strictly tourists. There was some regret to flying that far in her first trimester since morning sickness had become a thing, she'd said. But who would have expected that either? Kennedy had literally taken the test an hour before her wedding. Maybe had they stayed home she wouldn't be sick at all. Add time changes, altitude changes, and dietary differences, that would make anyone ill.

There was an added mark on the calendar she kept in her bathroom too. How many days it had been since she'd seen or heard from Chase.

Every mark only made it clearer to her that their truce, as it were, was the right thing to do. If she'd let him sweet talk her into something more, she'd have been disappointed when he didn't show or call. It would be expected, but it would have been disappointing all the same.

Paige had said that after Hillary had left the tap house that night she'd walked in with Max, that he and Chase had had a fight. Enough of a fight that Max had walked away with a bloodied lip.

She couldn't imagine what would have caused them to go to blows like that. They weren't like that. Well, there had been a few times, usually when they'd all been drinking. But that wasn't the case that night. She hadn't seen Max since then either, so she was just left in the dark like everyone else.

The coffee pot in the kitchen signaled that her coffee had been brewed. She took the towel from her wet hair, hung it on the hook, and went to sip on that warm jolt of energy.

Hillary sat at the kitchen table in the pink robe Kennedy had given her for Christmas a few years earlier with the matching fuzzy slippers that were keeping her feet warm.

She had turned the TV on to catch the weather and the traffic and nearly spilled her coffee down the front of her when the doorbell rang.

Looking at the clock above the microwave, it read seven-thirty a.m. Who in the world would be ringing her doorbell that early? She walked to the door and stood on her tip toes to look through the hole. Her heart began to hammer in her chest when she saw Chase out front and one of his limos parked on the street.

Hillary pulled open the door and a wall of frigid air blew at her.

"Hurry. Get in here," she demanded, pulling Chase by the arm. "It's freezing out there. And what are you doing here? Is everything okay? Are you okay? It's seven-thirty in the morning."

Chase smiled down at her and the cold that had rattled her melted away.

"God, you're beautiful in the morning. And I like your robe. A gift from my sister?"

Hillary laughed. "It all but has her name on it. What are you doing here?"

He held up a bag from a bakery. "I have croissants and a hole in my pants that I need mended. Kennedy isn't available, and I was hoping she made you mend things at work too. Can you help me out?"

"A hole in your pants?"

Chase opened his jacket and showed her the popped seam that ran from his crotch to the middle of his thigh. It would take her all of ten minutes to fix the hole, but he was going to have to take off his pants. She wasn't sure they could manage this very adult maneuver. She was naked under her robe, and in a minute, he'd be half naked in front of her.

"It won't take me but a second to fix that," she said trying to keep her voice steady.

"I brought in my gym shorts. I'll just change out of these."

He walked down the hall to her bathroom and shut the door.

Hillary let the air whoosh from her lungs before he returned. Unfortunately, she found it very sexy that he considered not just dropping his pants in front of her, because Chase Devereaux usually wouldn't have a problem with that.

When she heard the door open, she grabbed her sewing kit in the box her grandmother had handed down to her.

"How did you rip these?" she asked as he handed them to her and then turned to the bag of croissants he'd brought and pulled one out.

"I fell on the fricking ice. I haven't done that since I was ten. Wiped out on my ass right in front of my house."

Hillary lifted her head to study him. "Did you hurt yourself?"

"Just my pride," he offered with his mouth full of croissant. "Have you talked to my sister?"

"Yeah. She's getting morning sickness while she's there. But other than that, she's having an amazing time."

"What's the calendar in your bathroom? It looks like you've written hieroglyphics in it with a countdown."

Her eyes went wide when he mentioned it and she stabbed her finger with the needle. "Shit!"

Chase set the pastry down and hurried to her as she sucked the tiny bit of blood from her finger. He took her hand.

"You're bleeding."

"It'll stop in a moment." She pulled her hand, but he held on to it.

"I'm sorry. I've messed up your whole morning."

His fingers massaged her hand and distracted her from the task she'd been doing. "I'm all good." She managed to pull back her hand. "And you brought bakery goods, so no foul. Where are you headed anyway?"

"Airport. One of my regular clients is flying in with some business prospective buyers or something. I don't know. I have the bigger car; he pays me more money."

"Can't go wrong there."

"I'll have Kennedy paid off in no time. So, again, what's the calendar in your bathroom?"

Hillary winced knowing she'd left it on the counter, not that she'd expected anyone to go in there. Her calendar was as private as a diary. There were markings for periods, appointments, vacations, and sexual encounters. Had he flipped through it, or was it simply something to start a conversation? "Countdown to Mexico. Kennedy will be back in three days. Then I'll have a week before I can go on vacation."

Chase ran his hand over the back of his neck. "Mexico? By yourself?"

She nodded as she pulled the needle through the fabric. "It was supposed to be me and your sister, but she got distracted with men and babies."

"Yeah. Is it safe?"

Hillary didn't look up from her task. "Safe? You mean is it safe for a woman alone?"

"Okay. That's what I mean."

"It's a resort. It's like going to Vegas with a beach. I'll be fine. I just want to get out of this cold and get a tan." She finished knotting off the thread, put the needle into the cushion, and handed Chase the pants. "Good as new."

"God, I love you," he said, examining the pants. "You're a life saver."

She realized how easy it was for him to say those words. They never really had meant anything when he'd said them. Why had she put so much stock into it?

"I've got to get going." He turned and headed back to the bathroom as she put the sewing kit back together. When he returned, he looked as professional as he had when he walked in the door. "Let me take you to dinner as payment for this."

"It wasn't a big deal, Chase. You're going to be late."

"Seriously. Mexican at seven?"

Her lip began to twitch. "I have plans. But thank you."

His eyes saddened and he moved toward her again, so she quickly stood and tugged her robe tighter. "I really appreciate this. I owe you one."

Chase leaned in and kissed her cheek, just as Max had before they walked into the tap house.

He threw on his jacket. "There's three more pastries in that bag. Enjoy. Thanks again."

A moment later he was off, but Hillary braved the cold just to watch him climb into that big car and drive away. When he was out of sight, she shut the door and slid down it until she was on the floor. Her heart was in a million pieces. It wasn't good to want something so much.

CHAPTER 9

There was a break in the weather on Monday morning, and Hillary decided it was because Kennedy would be back in the store. Sunshine and Kennedy, it already was set to be a good day.

She walked from her car around the building to the front doors. There was something about those pink doors that welcomed anyone that walked through them. As she moved to open them, it opened from the other side and Joel walked out without holding the door open for her.

"Hey, I'm glad I caught you," he said, taking her by the arm and walking her away from the window. "She's having a really bad morning. We have a doctor's appointment this afternoon, but everything is making her sick. Just keep an eye on her. I brought her crackers, soup, water, and juice. She just can't keep it down."

"She should go home."

Joel laughed. "Right. You convince her of that."

"But the baby. Is the baby okay?"

His smile eased her. "It's just morning sickness and jet lag. I think she should take a few days off and get acclimated. She's worried about you and wants you to have some down time."

"That's stupid."

"She loves you, Hillary. She knows you have your vacation and wants you to be ready."

"I should cancel. I mean when I planned it, who knew that..."

"Who knew at all?" His smile beamed. "And if you canceled, she'd be devastated. Paige is going to help out."

"I'll keep an eye on her," Hillary promised.

Joel kissed her on the cheek. "I knew you would."

Hillary walked into the store and watched Kennedy emerge from the bathroom. Her skin was pale, and her hair hung around her face where normally it would bounce.

"You should go home," she said as she followed Kennedy into the break room and poured her a cup of apple juice. "There isn't a woman that will come in this store that doesn't understand what you're going through."

Kennedy pressed the back of her hand to her cheek. "I missed this. I want to be here."

"Then you're going to take it easy. Can I say you don't make pregnancy appealing?"

"It doesn't appeal to me either. My mom always said she was really sick with me and even sicker with Max."

"Men will do that to you," Hillary teased, and Kennedy laughed.

"Thanks for taking care of my brother while I was gone."

That sentence had Hillary stopping just short of the refrigerator and catching her breath.

As she pulled open the door, she let out a quiet breath. "What do you mean?"

"Chase told me you mended his pants for him. I have bought him a needle and black thread. I have shown him how to stitch his pants, but he refuses. He shows up at my house in the mornings and pulls off his pants or has me fix his jacket lining. It's something the man could do. But he said you helped him out. Now it's on you," she teased, and Hillary kept her back turned.

"Least I could do for your family, since they treat me like family."

"You're like a sister to all of us," she said and that made every muscle in Hillary's body tighten.

"I'd do anything for you all. You know that."

"I do. So, are you ready for your vacation?"

Hillary sat down in the chair across from Kennedy. "I am. I've been counting down. I've packed my suitcase three times. I think it'll be fun to have some alone time."

Kennedy shook her head before taking a sip of the juice. "I don't see you spending it alone. You'll find someone to hook up with."

Two weeks ago that comment would slide right off Hillary's shoulders, but now it hurt. Not that Kennedy meant anything by it.

"I think I'm ready to just enjoy the sun, some books, and sip margaritas I pay for."

"That doesn't sound like a Hillary vacation."

"It sounds like a *new* Hillary vacation. Don't worry about me. I'll have a great time."

Kennedy pressed her hands to the table. "I think it's time for round four." She stood up, waited, and then headed back to the bathroom.

"You should go home," Hillary shouted, but there was no reply.

CHASE VACUUMED out the limo and wiped down its interior. He couldn't wait until he could afford a garage to keep them all in. It would be so much easier to pull them in after use, do the maintenance, clean and vacuum them, and keep them safe from hail.

He had enough drivers that he could rotate through them and work the shifts or take the clients he wanted to. Maybe it was age, but he was finding he enjoyed taking the businessmen to the airport in the mornings more than he enjoyed the bachelorette parties.

Blame for that fell on Hillary. Not that it was her fault, but she was still occupying his mind three weeks after they'd hooked up.

Chase stepped out of the car just as another car pulled up in front of his house. He watched as the driver parked the car and stepped out. When it was the blonde from the tap house the night he punched Max, he dropped the rag on the floor of the car and shut the door.

"Hi," he said cautiously as she walked toward him.

"Amber," she reminded him, and he wasn't even sure she'd told him her name in the first place.

"Right. What can I do for you?"

She tucked her hands in the pockets of her coat and sauntered toward him. "I suppose you think this is really weird, me just showing up here?"

"I don't remember telling you where I live."

She bit down on her bottom lip. "You didn't. I know a girl who has been here, she told me where you live. You wouldn't have a beer, would you?"

Chase ran the back of his hand over his chin. "I might."

For the first time in his life, he felt out of his element. A month ago, he would have taken Amber home from the bar without knowing her name. Three weeks ago, he'd gotten her phone number. Now, he was like a deer in headlights wondering what the hell he was supposed to do with this woman who tracked him down.

It was guilt that was plaguing him. But what for? He wasn't seeing anyone. Nothing in his life had changed.

Life must go on, he reminded himself as Amber walked closer to him and he put his arm around her waist and escorted her into his house.

CHAPTER 10

C hecking her bag one more time, Hillary made sure she had everything she needed for her flight. Passport, check. Tickets, check. Gum, Tylenol, book, phone charger, check.

There had been some consideration of calling Chase and asking for a ride to the airport. She didn't need a limo, but she knew he'd be heading that way and she might as well fit in on one of his drives. But she thought better of it and decided to Uber instead. No one was put out that way, and she'd get to where she needed to be.

She'd called Kennedy three times already to make sure she was okay. The doctor had given her something for the nausea, and she was feeling much better. Besides, she had Paige to watch over her for a week. The rule was she wasn't to call back again until she was safely home. If need be, she could post a photo to Instagram of the ocean and her feet in the sand if she wanted people to know she was safe in Mexico.

Hillary had laughed that off, but that would be exactly what she'd do.

The Uber driver arrived and she was off on the vacation of a lifetime—alone.

It was no big deal, she kept telling herself. Everyone needed time to themselves. For the first time in her life she felt like a real adult. All decisions were hers for the next week, and she only had herself to answer to.

Butterflies flitted around in her stomach. She still worried about Kennedy, and until they'd announced that they were pulling away from the gate, she'd considered just staying.

Now she was in the air. There was nothing left to do but relax and enjoy her vacation.

$\sim$

SIX RIDES back and forth to the airport, and Chase was done being in a car. He'd taken Hillary's advice on some new podcasts and that mixed up his day a bit.

She'd been gone four days already and knowing she wasn't just around the corner had put him on edge.

The driver he'd hired recently had quit and he was put on the spot to be the driver for a bachelorette party that night. For the first time since he was old enough to drive, the thought of being in a car with eight sexy women did not appeal to him. There was nothing he wanted more than to stay home.

Of course, if he stayed home Amber might show up again. She'd been there six times in the past two weeks, and it was starting to feel as if she thought they were in a relationship.

In Chase's mind, nothing could be further from the truth. This was why one-night stands were so nice. One night and then it was over. Amber seemed to think that since she'd sought him out it meant they had more of a thing going.

It was his fault really, he kept letting her stay.

She'd rearranged his living room to have better feng shui, but he kept bumping into furniture that was out of place.

Maybe a good bachelorette party was just what he needed. He

could take one of them home and maybe Amber would show up and see that he was not interested.

THE PARTY HAD STARTED at a restaurant, then moved to a bar, and was now at an all male review. Chase stayed with the car, listening to podcasts and scrolling through the photos that Hillary was posting from her vacation.

A part of him wished he'd asked to go with her. But then that would have just ended up with them in bed together. A promise was a promise.

Just thinking about Hillary made it hard to sit in the car and breathe. Chase stepped outside of the car and rested against it.

"I hate these kinds of parties," the maid-of-honor walked toward him, removing her sash that announced her position in the wedding. "I have been a bridesmaid or maid-of-honor for six weddings in the past four years. We always end up drunk and at one of these places. Someone goes home with someone they're not supposed to, which then puts a damper on the wedding itself."

Chase chuckled. "I see it all the time. What did you do for your bachelorette party?"

The woman narrowed her gaze at him under the streetlamp light. "Always the bridesmaid, never the bride."

He figured, but sometimes it was good to get clarity even before starting a conversation.

"I can turn on the TV in the back if you'd like. There's plenty of alcohol as well. You could have your own party."

The woman slid right up next to him and leaned back on the car. "Whatcha looking at?"

Chase looked down at the phone and at a photo of Hillary in a bikini and large hat running toward the ocean. The part that bothered him about it was the fact that someone had to take the picture.

"Friend of mine is in Mexico on a solo vacation. I was just admiring her photos."

"Friend or girlfriend?"

An ache formed in his chest. "Friend. My sister's best friend."

"You're attached to her."

And didn't he know it. "Friend-zoned though. Story of our lives, right? Always the attendant?"

"Freaking sucks. Seriously how hard is it to find a nice guy? You know, I work in a hospital. I'm a trauma nurse. I'm surrounded by all those guys that moms hope their daughters marry. Those first responder types, doctors, you know? And they're all self-absorbed." She let out a breath. "I'm Tammi by the way," she held out her hand and Chase took it, choosing to kiss it rather than shake it.

"Chase."

"Is that your real name or your job designation. You know, chaser of women?" She playfully raised her eyebrows.

"Actual name."

"Well, Chase, what movies do you have in this thing? Anything edgy?"

"I could find something for you."

She moved in closer, turning to face him, and wrapping her leg around his. "Why don't you join me back here and we could watch something together."

He looked down at his phone. The next photo of Hillary was her sitting in a lounge chair laughing with a drink in her hand. She was having a good time with someone and he needed to get her out of his head.

"I think we have some time. Club doesn't close until two."

She placed her hand on his chest. "After that, I'd be happy to make you breakfast, if you'd be interested."

Chase reached around her and opened the door. "I'd be interested."

CHAPTER 11

Chase had managed to inquire about Hillary's itinerary enough that he knew when she'd be landing and making it through customs. Hopefully his sister didn't know what he was doing by prying. He felt the need to be there when she got home.

Tammi had gone home with him Friday night, and she'd stayed all weekend. He'd found he really enjoyed her company. Not only did it take his mind off Hillary for a few days, it got the point across to Amber that he wasn't the kind of guy who kept just one woman, even if she moved his furniture around.

However, Tammi seemed to fill a need in a way no other woman had, and Hillary refused to.

But the draw to see Hillary was still there, and he decided the only way to overcome it was to see her in person.

Checking the monitors, he found her flight and the status. It had landed, so it was just a matter of time before she walked through the secure doors.

As he would with any client, he had a sign with her name on it, but he also had a bouquet of flowers—daisies, which were her favorites.

When people began walking through the doors, he waited. His palms had gone damp and his stomach fluttered at the thought of seeing her. It had only been a week, and he'd gone much longer than that before. But this time it was different—they were different, and yet they were still only friends.

When he did see her, she'd walked right past him and straight for the bathroom. How did she not see him standing there?

He waited, and when she walked out of the bathroom, he called her name to avoid her missing him again. But she didn't look quite right.

She lifted her eyes to meet his, but they were sunken and dark. Her skin was pale and there was no sign of sun basking at all.

Hillary mustered a smile. "Hey," she said, but even her words were drawn out. "What are you doing here?"

"I thought it would be a nice surprise to pick you up. What the hell is wrong with you?"

She leaned against him as he wrapped his arm around her shoulder. "Too much of a good thing, I guess."

"I guess." His gut twisted harder now. So this was what it looked like when you'd gone on a bender for a week? According to her pictures, which someone else obviously took, what else would he think. "The car is just out front. Why don't you sit and let me swing around to get you?"

"That would be really nice. Thanks."

She was sick, he decided. Hillary would rather sprint through the parking lot to prove that she didn't need special treatment. This wasn't like her.

He helped her to a seat and hurried to the car. She was sitting with her head propped up against the wall, eyes closed, and looking paler than when he'd left her.

"C'mon," he helped her to her feet.

"Can I sit in the front? I'd rather sit by you," she asked, and he opened the passenger door.

Once she was situated, he reached in the back, pulled out a cold bottle of water and opened it for her.

"Here, I think you need this. Maybe you drank too much."

She only nodded and sipped the water.

When he'd decided to pick her up, he thought he'd convince her to go for lunch. He just wanted to get a feel for where things were before he spent another week with Tammi, because that was heavy on his mind too.

Now, he just wanted to get her home and tucked into bed.

"You look like shit," he said as he pulled into traffic. "But did you have fun?"

When she didn't answer, he shifted his glance to notice she'd fallen asleep.

He deserved this. She'd spent an entire week on a beach, drinking, not sleeping, and heaven knows who she'd been with. She was a party girl, just like he was a party guy. They'd hooked up for that reason. To think there was more to it would only keep him up nights.

At a stop light, he pulled out his phone and checked his messages. There were three from Tammi.

"Who is Tammi?" the weak voice came from Hillary.

"You can't keep your eyes open, but you can focus on a name in my phone?"

She shrugged, closing her eyes again. "Just asked."

What did he tell her? For all she knew, Tammi was a client. But they'd never lied to each other before. Then again, they'd never had reason to.

"She's a girl I'm seeing."

The light turned green and he didn't see her reaction, if any, because she didn't say another word the entire drive.

When he got to her house, he pulled the keys from her purse, unlocked the door, and then went back to help her out of the car.

He helped to her bed, and when he took off her shoes and lifted her sweater off her, she didn't even seem to care.

After retrieving her luggage and making sure she had water and crackers by her bedside, he left.

Before replying back to Tammi, he called Kennedy.

"Hillary is home."

"How do you know that? She didn't call me yet."

He sighed into the phone. "Because I went and picked her up. I thought it would be a nice surprise."

"Was it?" she asked without suspicion.

"I don't think so. Listen, she's really sick. I mean really sick. She's pale, lethargic, and weak. I don't think she slept the entire week. She probably has alcohol poisoning or something. When you get a chance, I think you should head over there."

"You just left her alone?"

Of course he did. The last person Hillary needed was him, he thought. "Ken, I have things to do. I have another client to pick up."

"Then why did you go in the first place?"

"Seriously, the issue here is that Hillary is sick. We need to get her to a doctor or get her electrolytes up. It's Monday, you don't have appointments, and I'm not being a shit about it. Tell Paige to watch the store and go check on her, please."

"Okay. Okay. I'll go. Thanks for picking her up. I'm sure she'll be grateful when she feels better."

But Chase wasn't sure she would.

CHAPTER 12

Hillary heard noises coming from her kitchen. She pried her eyes open and took in the sight of her dark bedroom. The blinds had been pulled tight and her door had been closed.

Next to her was a glass of water, a plate of crackers, and a vase full of daisies.

Daisies?

Chase had those with him when he'd picked her up at the airport.

She smiled. He'd picked her up at the airport.

Then the question stirred in her head. Why?

Because they were friends, and she needed to remember that. Friends would do things like that for each other. Especially friends who loved each other.

Again, she heard something coming from the kitchen. Maybe he was there. Wouldn't that be nice? She'd enjoy sitting with him and just being normal. She owed him one for taking such good care of her. That flight had really jostled her up. Of course, she'd been sick most of the week, and when she was feeling better, she was dizzy. Who the hell goes to Mexico and drinks only one margarita? Or half of one, as the case was. She had to have gotten sick, like so many tourists did, on the first day. What a waste of a vacation.

But no one, but she, was the wiser for it. On that first day, she'd put on her bikini and wide brimmed hat and headed down to the beach. She'd ordered that margarita and asked the woman in the bungalow next to her to take some photos. She ran toward the ocean, sipped from the margarita, laughed, and lounged. The woman took twenty shots that looked like one amazing vacation when she went back through them.

Each day when she wasn't feeling so well, she'd post one. Maybe when she looked back on it, she'd only remember that it was a spectacular time. She might have gotten away with that story in its entirety too, had Chase not picked her up.

She looked at the daisies again.

But he had picked her up. What an amazing friend.

Hillary eased her legs over the edge of the bed and gave it a moment to make sure she could stand. Already she felt better having slept in her bed. Knowing Chase was in her kitchen, that made her feel even better.

She opened the door and walked down the hallway. The TV was on, and she could hear the news anchor talking. She'd slept for a long time, she decided.

When she turned the corner, Kennedy smiled up at her. "You don't look as horrible as he said you did. You must have gotten some rest."

Hillary wondered if the disappointment of seeing her best friend standing in her kitchen was evident. "I looked that bad, huh?"

"Chase thought so. How do you feel?"

Hillary shrugged as she balanced herself with the back of the chair as she pulled it out and sat down. "I'm okay. What do they call that? Montezuma's revenge?"

"Something like that. But it looked like you had an amazing time."

Now it was her story, and that's all that mattered. "I did. Thanks for the time off."

"Are you kidding me? You deserved it. You've been running the show for a month or more. I mean, maniac bridezilla."

Hillary laughed. "You were not. In fact, I think you handled it much better than I thought you would. By the way. How do you feel?"

"I feel much better. The doctor gave me some nausea medicine and I've kept everything down. In fact, I've gained six pounds. I'm only eight weeks pregnant. I'm going to be the size of a house."

"And who will that matter to? No one."

Kennedy sat two mugs of hot water down on the table and a plate of tea bags, then sat across from Hillary. "Joel says he doesn't care what I look like during or after this pregnancy. He's elated. I mean crazy elated."

"He loves you so much."

Kennedy sighed. "He does. I'm a very lucky girl and I know it. Now all we need to do is find you a man. Did you meet one or two in Mexico?"

There was a slight jab there, but Hillary deserved that due to her track record, so she wasn't going to be offended by its innocent delivery.

"Nope. I just enjoyed my peace."

"It looks like someone took those photos."

"Doesn't mean I hooked up with them or got to know them," she said. "Just someone who offered to take the picture."

Kennedy ripped the paper off a peppermint tea bag and dunked it into her water. "Disappointing. I wanted gossip. But I'm glad you had fun."

Hillary picked up a peppermint bag as well and ripped the paper off it. "So, Chase is seeing someone?"

Kennedy lifted her head and her brows drew inward. "My brother Chase?"

"I don't know another one."

"Seeing someone? That means that he'd have seen the same person more than one night. That's weird."

Her explanation of it landed in Hillary's gut. "Yeah. Seeing someone means dating, right?"

"I guess so. Good for him. I didn't think he had it in him," Kennedy said as she lifted her mug to her lips and blew. "I'd like to see him fall in love and settle down. I think it would do a lot of good for him."

"I didn't say he'd fallen in love."

"Well, no. I just think it would be nice for him. His idea of family is more skewed than mine. I mean his married mother had an affair with my married father and had him. He has siblings all over the place, and yet his parents were never married. It's so sad. His idea of love it to spread it all over the place."

The nausea that had plagued Hillary was back, but she knew it was because Kennedy was right. The fact that he told her he loved her meant nothing. He didn't understand love and commitment. Whoever Tammi was, she would probably find that out.

CHAPTER 13

Hillary gave it a few days before going back to work. She was sure Paige had had her fill of working with her sister and wanted to get back to her own life.

Whatever had plagued her in Mexico had eased.

She stopped by the bakery on her way in and ordered a pastry, but the cinnamon rolls were looking mighty tempting. So, she bought both. Surely Kennedy, in her delicate state, would want to share with her.

When she reached the front door, she reached inside her purse for her keys. Just as she pulled them out, the door opened and Chase stepped out, startled that she was standing there.

"Hey," he said, and smiled as he tucked his hands into the front pockets of his jeans.

"Hey. You look casual today. No rides to the airport?"

He took his sunglasses off the top of his head and slid them on. "No. Took a few days off to head to the lake."

"It's thirty degrees," she reminded him, and he laughed.

"Right. Um, Tammi, has a friend who has a cabin up there. She's letting us have it for a few days."

Hillary forced a smile to her lips, hoping that it looked

genuine. "That sounds like a really nice time. You're serious about this woman, huh?"

Chase ran his hand over the back of his neck. "It's been two weeks. But I enjoy her company."

"Right. Vacations with strangers. That's your new norm."

"Hillary..." His voice had dipped.

"Hey, you don't owe me any explanations. We're just friends, right?"

"Right." He rocked back on his heels. "I know you had a good time in Mexico. That's all that mattered."

The forced smile began to ache in her cheeks. "That's right. Amazing time in Mexico. The stories..." She dropped the keys back in her purse. "For another time. Hey, have a great vacation at the lake. Don't walk out on the ice. Wear a condom. Make good choices. You know, all the stuff."

As she took a step toward the door, he reached for her arm.

"I'm glad you're feeling better."

Smile still in place, she nodded. "Just too much fun in Mexico."

The conversation ended there, as Hillary opened the door to the store and stepped inside.

"Asshole," she murmured under her breath.

"What?" Kennedy looked up at her as did Max who was standing on the back side of the counter with his sister.

"Nothing. I have pastries. I hope you'll share them with me. I went for one and ended up with more than that because they all looked so good."

Max lifted his chin. "I'll help you eat them," he offered with a grin.

"Good. I'll go plate them."

She walked to the break room and Kennedy and Max followed, each taking a seat at the table. Hillary shrugged out of her coat and hung it on the hook.

She watched them assemble as she pulled down a plate. "What are you guys working on?"

Kennedy turned her head to look at her. "Max is going to help me do a little remodeling. We're going to build some space into my office so we can have a little nursery. I figure with Joel next door, and me here, there's no reason for us to have the baby in daycare or anything like that. I know it won't be easy, but his mother has already asked for two days a week. So, I figure if I have the baby here on Monday with me, I don't have clients. I'll build my client schedule around his work schedule, and I'll make sure I have down times when the baby is here. This is going to work."

Her enthusiasm was contagious.

"Sounds nice." She set the plate on the table and took the third chair. "When are you starting?"

Max turned the drawings toward her so she could see them. "It'll be a few weeks, a month maybe. I'm knee-deep in a project right now. I want to be focused on it so I can get it done as quickly, and as nicely, as I can," he said smiling at his sister, who rested a hand on his arm.

"God, I'm lucky to have talented people around me."

"Yeah, well, wait till you get my bill," he joked, and she pinched his arm. "That's extra."

Hillary tore off a piece of the cinnamon roll and popped it in her mouth. She'd been right to get it. It was amazing.

"This is going to be really nice, Ken," Hillary said looking at the plans that Max had laid on the table.

"I hope so," she agreed as she took a piece of the cinnamon roll and moaned as she tasted it. "I'm surprised I've had a business near that bakery this long and I haven't gained fifty pounds."

"Now's the time, right?" Hillary teased.

"Shut your mouth," Kennedy scolded as she took another bite. "So, what did you say when you walked in the door? I saw you talking to Chase."

Hillary licked the frosting from her fingers. "I think I said asshole," she repeated matter-of-factly.

Max snorted a laugh. "Did he make a crass comment? You wouldn't be the first woman I heard say that under her breath about him."

"It's not important. Chase is usually an asshole."

"Isn't that the truth?" Max agreed as he ripped the other pastry in half and took a bite.

Kennedy elbowed Max. "You guys have another argument?"

"We argue all the time. But yeah, a few weeks ago we had a doozie."

"I need gossip," Kennedy said taking another bite of cinnamon roll. "Spill it."

Hillary noticed the glance that shifted her way before he turned his attention back to Kennedy. "Misunderstanding one night while you were in Paris. He was working at the tap house, I came in. He got something in his mind, and we agreed to go outside to hash it out. Instead, he came at me with those stupid meat hooks and clocked me in the jaw. I knocked him on his ass and got the last punch in. Five minutes tops and we walked back inside with our arms around each other and he bought me a beer. 'Nuff said," he finished by taking the rest of the pastry and shoving it in his mouth.

Kennedy shook her head, obviously not surprised by the news. "Some day he's going to talk himself into something he can't talk his way out of. I love him, but he needs to grow up."

Hillary wiped her fingers on a paper towel. "Isn't it grown up to go out of town with a new girlfriend?" she asked, making sure to keep her voice steady.

Kennedy snorted. "Two weeks with one girl is not a commitment. But we'll see. I suppose if you pick up a new bridesmaid each week, sooner or later one will want to be the bride."

Hillary felt the color drain from her cheeks, and she knew Max had seen it too.

As he gathered up the papers, Kennedy pushed herself away from the table. "I know pregnant women go to the bathroom a lot, but this baby isn't even the size of a tomato and I'm in there all the time."

Max shook his head. "Too much information."

Kennedy kissed him on the top of the head. "I love you. Thank you for doing this."

"My pleasure."

Hillary watched as Kennedy disappeared and Max headed for the door. Quickly, she grabbed her coat and followed him out of the store.

"Hey," she called, closing the door behind her.

Max turned around. "Did I forget something?"

"No. I just was curious, was your fight with Chase over me?"

Max let out a long breath that carried on the cold air. "Listen, I didn't know about you two. I was only being nice, and I didn't mean to start anything by walking in with you the way I did or buying you a drink."

Hillary rested her hand on his arm. "There is nothing between us."

"He told me that."

"I'm so sorry he punched you. God, he is an asshole."

Now Max laughed. "The biggest asshole I know. But I love him. And you're okay with this girlfriend thing?"

"We said it was just a night. So, it was just a night."

Max wrinkled up his face. "That's not convincing, Hill. And for what it's worth, I think it meant more to him than that. Now, this is Chase we're talking about, so take that with a grain of salt. Anyway, there was no gossip. Kennedy doesn't know. I won't say a word to anyone about it."

"I really appreciate that."

He leaned in and kissed her on the cheek. "Anything for you."

CHAPTER 14

C hase looked out over the frozen lake from the balcony off the bedroom. Dressed in jeans and boots, he'd thrown on his coat and walked outside to sit in the cold while Tammi lounged in a bubble bath. He had to admit it was beautiful. The lake was snow-covered, but he knew from experience that didn't mean it was frozen through. He'd forever be grateful for his brother for being quick to pull him out of that mess when they were fourteen. It was just one of many secrets he and Max would take to their graves.

Max, he owed a lot to him. He'd financed his first car when Kennedy wouldn't lend him the money. He'd pulled him out of frozen lakes and picked him up from numerous bars. Since they were kids, Max owned him as a brother when his other brothers and sisters thought he was a bastard. Well, those who shared his last name never treated him like that. No, for the mess of a family they were, his Devereaux side was tight.

His mother's other children, his two older brothers and his younger sister and brother, didn't have much to do with him.

Oh, his mom came around when she was having a guilt trip

63

over his existence, which still happened after thirty-six years. But, day to day, she didn't pay too much attention to what he did.

His father was currently having his own drama after having had a heart attack on a cruise. He'd found a woman on that cruise, and she was nice enough. It made Chase consider the fact that he didn't call his dad as often as he should. Maybe when his father got home, he'd see if he wanted to meet for a beer. Even though the circumstances surrounding Chase's existence weren't honorable, his father had stepped up and kept all of his children together—as a family—even if they lived in different homes. He owed it to him to pay a little attention to him.

Chase's thoughts circled back to Max. He worked his ass off, and Chase wondered if he'd ever settle down. Out of all of them, he was most likely to find a wife and have kids. It surprised him that he hadn't.

There had been one woman, and she'd been the love of Max's life. But big dreams were hard to give up for love without the promise of security. She'd gone on to pursue those dreams, and Max stayed behind to work on building that security for someone else—but no one else had ever taken her place.

Of course, when his brother had a moment with a nice girl, Chase took him outside and kicked the shit out of him. Okay, he reconsidered, Max had held his own and it was Chase that had the shit kicked out of him—all over Hillary.

Kennedy probably wouldn't bat an eye if it were Max that had taken Hillary home. She'd have known Hillary was taken care of, and probably for life. That stability was set now, and Max was a long-term guy—unlike Chase who only had a reputation for loving and leaving.

"What are you doing out here, handsome?" Tammi's voice came from the doorway behind him.

He turned to see her wrapped in a blanket with a towel still on her head.

"I was just taking in the scenery and thinking."

"Thinking about what?"

"My family."

Tammi tiptoed over the snow and fell into his lap laughing. "That's not sexy at all," she told him as she pressed a kiss to his neck. "Why don't you think about something else."

Her mouth came to his and for a moment he forgot that he was feeling bad for punching his brother in a jealous fit.

AFTER A FEW DAYS at the lake house with Tammi, Chase felt rejuvenated. He picked up a few shifts at the tap house, which he found invigorating, and from that he'd booked the limo for a fortieth birthday party and a wedding. Joel had been right about the connection and opportunity he'd get out of working there.

It also gave him reason to look outside and see Hillary's car and know she was close.

Tammi sat at the bar, closest to his station. He'd tried to gently tell her that he'd be working and wouldn't have time for much conversation, but she insisted on hanging out. A part of him said that she was keeping an eye on him. A different part thought she was just happy to be around people. Either way, he didn't like it. He wasn't going fishing for phone numbers, not with Tammi in the picture. But hell, she seduced him into the limo after having just learned his name, so he could see why she might think he mightn't turn anyone away.

As he filled an order, he saw his sister walk through the back door. Looking up at the clock he realized it was six-thirty. She would have closed the store, done the books, and cleaned the bathroom. And Hillary would have headed home.

"Hey, I didn't know you were working tonight," she moved around the bar and gave him a squeeze with one arm as he balanced two glasses under taps.

"They needed someone for a few nights. I'm the go to."

"I like it."

He realized that Tammi had perched up on her stool, and he was obligated to introduce her to his sister.

"Hey, Kennedy, this is Tammi," he said as he nodded in her direction and set the beers on the tray.

"Oh, it's nice to meet you." Kennedy moved around the bar and extended her manicured hand toward Tammi. "Chase mentioned you."

"Thank you. I love your bracelet and that color polish."

Chase let out a sigh. "Here we go."

Both eyes turned toward him. "Go sit at a table and tell her about the jewelry and the signature pink. I have things to do."

They laughed and Kennedy escorted Tammi to table in the back corner.

A few minutes later, when he looked up, he noticed Hillary walk in the back door with a box in her arms, trying hard to negotiate the mat at the doorway in her high heels. He hurried to her and took the box.

"Let me help you with that," he offered.

"Thanks. The delivery guy set it in front of our door without even looking at the label. It belongs over here."

"Thanks. Can I buy you a drink?"

She chuckled at that. "Very sweet of you, but I'll pass."

"Kennedy is here. You could stay a while."

"No. I think I'll go home and get to bed early. I'm extremely tired today."

"Are you feeling okay? I know after Mexico..."

"Oh, yeah. I'm good. Maybe it's the winter blahs," she said as a woman walked up to them as if she were part of the conversation.

She held out her hand. "I'm Tammi."

Hillary slid her hands into her coat because they'd begun to shake. "The girlfriend?" she asked, shifting a glance to Chase and then back to Tammi. "It's nice to meet you. I'm Hillary. I work with Kennedy."

Tammi retracted her hand. "Oh, you missed her. She just left with her husband."

"I was delivering a package. Anyway, you two have a lovely night and I'm sure I'll see you around."

HILLARY HURRIED BACK out the door, careful not to catch her heels on the ice, but all she wanted to do was run. He deserved to find someone that didn't turn him away, but all Hillary wanted to do was rip that woman's hair out. She was out of sorts, and over Chase Devereaux.

She never would have stayed the night had she known she'd would be twisted up over it for weeks. This wasn't how it was the first time.

But the night of the wedding was different from the start. From the moment she'd seen him standing at the alter with Joel as she walked down the aisle, to slow dances, drinks, and the soft whispers in her ear. The moment he swayed toward her, she caught him, and he'd kissed her—she was a goner. When he leaned over at the stoplight and pressed a kiss to her neck, making her linger there with her eyes closed until the car behind them honked, the thought of it still made her heart flutter.

God, they almost hadn't made it out of the car when she'd parked in his driveway. How come she could recount every movement through the house that night? Why couldn't she have forgotten it like she assumed Chase had.

The very thought that it meant so much more to her had her body shaking.

Before she could make it between the buildings, her stomach roiled and she found herself throwing up in a bush. This wasn't like her at all. Had he really gotten her so worked up?

CHAPTER 15

"The snow has all melted, and did you see the tulips in the planters coming up?" Kennedy walked through the front door of the store carrying three bouquets from the florist down the street.

"What are you doing?" Hillary pushed herself off the floor where she'd been tagging merchandise. "Did you buy out the store?"

Kennedy laid the flowers on the counter. "I'm so ready for spring. I just want the snow gone and flowers to bloom." She stood back from the counter and looked at her purchase, resting her hands on the tautness of her belly.

Hillary thought it was cute, but if someone didn't know she was pregnant they'd have no idea.

"I'll get some vases. Those new purses are adorable."

"Aren't they? They were the first things I ordered from Paris this year," she said, and Hillary heard the bell over the door chime.

She pulled down the vases as she heard Kennedy talking to the customer that had walked in.

With the three vases in her arms, she walked around the corner to see Tammi standing there with Kennedy. One of the vases slid from her hands and crashed to the floor shattering into a thousand pieces.

"Dear Lord! Are you okay?" Kennedy asked as she took a step toward her.

"Don't you move. You just stay there," Hillary warned. "It just slipped out of my hands. I'll make sure to replace it."

"Don't be stupid. We have many more."

Tammi took a step toward Hillary and held out her hand to take the other vases.

"Thank you."

"No problem. I break things all the time," she said as she set the vases on the counter. "I have broken three plates at Chase's in the past three weeks." She laughed and it triggered tears to well in Hillary's eyes. What was that about?

"I'll get a broom. No one move," she warned again as she hurried to the break room

As she passed by the dressing room, she noticed her reflection. The dark circles under her eyes did not look good with that dress, she teased herself mentally. It was no wonder she'd dropped the vase. She was just so tired.

Hillary hurried back to the showroom and began sweeping up the shards of glass. Tammi quickly offered to help, but Hillary shook her head at the offer.

"Nope, I've got this. You came in for a reason, and this certainly wasn't it."

"Actually, one of Chase's clients is having some big dinner. Black tie. He says they invite him every year."

Hillary swallowed hard. "At the Saint Pierre?"

Tammi's eyes grew wide. "Yes."

"It's a nice little shindig. I went with him a few years ago." She felt the need to clear her throat, especially when Kennedy's eyes narrowed. "Anyway, you're in the right place for a dress. I'd steer away from purple though. The owner's wife wears purple all the time, and it's kind of an unwritten rule that no one else wears purple."

"Thanks."

Kennedy eased around the counter. "C'mon, let's see what I have in the back."

Hillary was grateful that she'd hurried Tammi away. Of course, he'd take his girlfriend to the event. Hillary hadn't expected an invitation. He'd taken many other girls to it after they had gone to the party years ago—and ended up in bed together.

Hillary began to sweep up the glass that lay on the floor. Those tears that had threatened earlier now were fresh and clogging her throat. She needed to get the mess cleaned up and get a grip. Why was she so freaking emotional? It wasn't as if Chase hadn't had his share of women after they hooked up the first time, and she'd moved on just as quickly. Why was it so hard this time?

The tears fell, and she cursed herself. Was she going to need therapy? Never in her entire life had she been so worked up over something—or someone. It was starting to affect every aspect of her life.

She heard Tammi's laugh from the other room, and the tears fell harder. Something was seriously wrong with her.

When the door opened again, Chase walked into the store dressed in his uniform. His eyes went wide when he saw Hillary on her knees trying to sort through the bigger shards of glass.

"HOLY SHIT. That wasn't some expensive vase was it?" he asked and watched as Hillary looked up at him, her eyes filled with tears and mascara running down her cheeks. "Sweetheart, are you hurt?"

"Shhh," she scolded. "Just don't worry about me. I need to get this cleaned up."

"Where is Kennedy?"

"In the back with Tammi. I don't want either of them to see me like this."

"Let me help you." He took the broom from her hand and swept up the glass on the floor. "If you're worried about Kennedy, she's not going to care that you broke this. Why are you crying?"

"Why don't you just leave me alone and let me take care of this?"

He stood there with the broom and watched as she dropped the big pieces into the trash can. Never, in all of the years he'd known her had he seen her so moody. He was worried about her.

Hillary picked up another large piece of glass, and it fell from her hand causing her to instinctively try and catch it. Instantly she jumped back, blood dripping from her palm.

Chase dropped the broom and ran to her. A large shard of glass stuck out from her hand and she swayed back and forth.

"You need stitches," he said and held her as her face drained of color.

He pulled the glass from her hand. "Kennedy! Get out here."

Kennedy hurried out and held on to the counter as she saw the blood dripping from Hillary's hand.

"Pull yourself together. Get a towel. I'm going to take her to the urgent care and get this stitched up. I need you to buck up and not pass out on me, too."

Kennedy nodded her head and ran for a towel. She returned a moment later and held out the towel without looking. When had all the women in his life become so weak?

Wrapping the towel around Hillary's hand, he eased her to her feet.

"Where is Tammi?"

"She's in the dressing room."

"Okay. Tell her what happened, and I'll call her later. I'm going to get this stitched up for her and then take her home."

Kennedy nodded and Chase eased Hillary out of the store and into his car.

CHAPTER 16

Hillary held the towel around her hand as Chase drove toward the emergency care center only a few miles away.

He shifted his glance to her and couldn't believe how pale she was. "Seriously, are you okay?"

"Just get me there. I'm freaking out."

He sped through the yellow light and continued on. "I have seen you fall, get in fights, and go head over handlebars on a bike. When did you get so queasy around blood?"

"I don't know. Just drive. I don't need your help beyond this."

The tears were back, and he hadn't wanted to do that to her. "Do you think you got poisoned in Mexico?"

She snapped her head to the side to look at him. "Are you nuts? What the hell kind of question was that?"

"You were just so sick getting off the plane and you're just not yourself."

"That was three weeks ago. This was an accident."

"But you're all worked up over it."

"Maybe that's because you keep showing up and getting in my face."

Chase pulled into the parking lot of the urgent care center. He put the car in park and skirted the front to open the door for her. Without her getting too upset, he eased her out of the car and helped her inside.

He was pleased that they took her directly back and put her in a room.

"You can go. I'll get someone to come and get me," she argued as she got situated in the room.

"How about you let me stay? I help fill out this paperwork they need from you, and I take you home when you're done. If you need a ride in the morning, I'll pick you up and take you to work."

"You don't have to treat me like a child."

"You're acting like a child." He flipped through the pages on the clipboard he held in his hand. "Are you going to help me fill these out?"

She growled, and he was humored by it, but he didn't laugh. Instead, he began to fill out the questions on the sheet, only needing to ask for a few items he didn't know about her family history. Otherwise, he knew her as well as she knew herself.

It still took nearly an hour and a half to get her hand stitched up and release her.

As he had before, he helped her to the car and latched her seat belt.

HILLARY TURNED her head as Chase leaned in over her and fastened her belt. It didn't stop her from inhaling his cologne. She let her eyes close as the feeling of him being near washed over her. There were no other words spoken between them as he drove toward her house. What would she say? The emotional rollercoaster she was on was exhausting.

When he came to a stop in front of her house, she rolled her head to the side to face him.

"Thank you for taking care of me. That was just a freak thing."

He smiled at her. "Tammi texted when they were bandaging you up. She hopes you're okay."

Did she, Hillary wondered. "I'll be fine. Thanks for the ride home."

Chase stepped out of the car and walked around to open her door. He helped her out and started toward the front door with her purse in his hand.

"Do I have permission to look for your key?" he asked.

"Yes."

She watched as he fished through her purse, coming up with her ring of keys. He slid the key into the lock and pushed open the door.

"They said to keep your hand elevated for the night. Where do you want to set up?"

"Seriously, you can go."

"And seriously, you can let me help you." He tossed her purse on the chair and followed her to the sofa where she finally sat down.

He took the throw pillows off the sofa and created her a place to rest her arm.

"Where are your medicines? Tylenol? Motrin?"

"Bathroom cabinet."

CHASE MOVED to the bathroom and opened the cabinet. There were small bottles of allergy medicines, antacids, and pain medications. Of course, there was the expected case of birth control pills. Seeing them there took him back to the day after they were together when he realized he'd never found a condom. There was some solace in knowing she was taken care of.

He poured two Motrin in his hand and walked back to her.

"Do you still keep bottles of fancy water in your fridge?"

She chuckled. "Yes. Healthy obsession?"

"If you say so."

Chase retrieved a bottle of fizzy water from her refrigerator and sat down next to her on the couch, opening the bottle and handing it to her after she popped the two pills into her mouth.

"Thank you."

He took the water from her and set it on the table. "My pleasure. I left the instructions they sent in your purse. I'll be here at eight o'clock in the morning to take you to work," he offered, holding up his hand to ward off her rejection of the idea, but she didn't say anything. "Other than not getting your hand wet, you should be okay to continue on with your life."

Hillary rested her head back against the couch. "Thank you. You're always there for me when I need you."

Chase looked at her eyes, finally dry and kind. He brushed a strand of hair from her forehead and lingered his hand there for a moment. "I will always be here for you. You know that."

"I do. By the way, Tammi seems nice."

Tammi. How easy it was to let Tammi slip from his mind when he was with Hillary.

"Yeah. She's great. She's just kinda stuck around."

Hillary's brows rose. "And you don't mind that? That's not your style."

He shrugged. "Guess I was in the mood for company, ya know?"

"Yeah. Well, I think I'm good here. I'll be ready when you get here at eight."

He sat for a moment searching her eyes for a sign—any sign that he should kiss her goodnight. But it never came. In fact, he knew he needed to walk away, or he'd forever make a mess of things with her.

"I'll see you in the morning," he said as he stood and walked out of the house.

The evening air offered enough cool air that he inhaled deeply attempting to calm his mind.

It had been nearly two months since their night together. He needed to forget all about it.

CHAPTER 17

The store was quiet, and Hillary was grateful for that. Kennedy and Joel had gone to their doctor appointment, and Hillary had already stocked all the items that had shipped in that day.

Because Kennedy wasn't around for an hour, she'd also put up the sign that said she'd be back in ten minutes and walked down to the bakery for a cinnamon roll, which had become her habit lately.

With spring's arrival, she thought she'd take Paige up on the offer to attend a few of her yoga classes and maybe she'd even consider walking to work. It was less than four miles, and she once ran track, it would come back to her.

As she licked the last crumb off her finger, the front door opened, and Hillary heard the familiar voices of Kennedy and Joel. A moment later, as she threw away any evidence that she'd indulged in the decadent treat, they walked into the break room.

"You have to see what I have," Kennedy squealed as she waved a piece of paper in the air. "Look. Look!"

"You have to hold still," Hillary laughed, taking the paper from her hands. She studied it. "This is an ultrasound, right? This is your baby?"

Kennedy beamed and tears formed in her eyes.

Joel wrapped his arm around her shoulders. "The baby is growing perfectly, and Kennedy is doing great. We are right at twelve weeks. The baby is due October thirteenth."

Watching Kennedy tear up over the baby made Hillary tear up too. Seriously, this new emotional baggage, whatever it was, was getting out of hand.

"I'm so happy for you," Hillary said batting away tears. "You're going to be wonderful parents. I can't wait to meet him, or her."

"I can't either. Max said he can start on the nursery in a few weeks. And then we're going to have him come to the house and remodel the basement so that I can put my jewelry studio down there and we can finish the nursery at the house."

"What a year, huh? Things are changing around here so fast. Cara finally gets pregnant, and now she's having a set of twins on top of that. You're having a baby. I'm going to start bringing in that fizzy flavored water that I drink, because the water around here is tainted."

Kennedy pulled her in for a hug. "I love you. I couldn't do this if you weren't here to help me. I'm going to be slacking so much."

"You're the boss. You're allowed to slack."

"Yeah, but you're not exclusively supposed to pick it all up."

Joel moved in and kissed Kennedy on the cheek. "I have to get back to work. Love you both. Take care of each other," he said before walking out the back door and across the lot to the tap house.

"I'm still seriously in awe of the two of you. Who would have thought you'd find a man, get married and pregnant?"

"It wasn't in my plan. So, did the last of the dresses make it in from Paris?"

Hillary nodded, suddenly feeling the effects of the cinnamon roll in her stomach. "I hung them in the back. They need to be steamed."

Kennedy's eyes grew wide. "Let's go try them on."

"I'm game, but you're a different size," Hillary joked.

"I'm not going to wear any. You are. I want to see them. C'mon," she said taking Hillary's hand and heading to the dressing room in back.

Kennedy always made sure to buy outfits in sizes that she and Hillary could wear. Then two that were smaller and two that were larger. At any given time, there should be no more than five people wearing that same outfit in the entire metro area.

Kennedy touched each of the dresses and fawned over them. Hillary loved to watch her, she truly enjoyed what she did.

"Let's do this one first," she said holding up a black strappy number. "I can see you waltzing into the ball room of the Saint Pierre in this number."

Certainly, Kennedy hadn't used that example to make Hillary feel worse than she did about Chase taking Tammi to the event. But seeing that Kennedy moved right on to the accessories she wanted Hillary to try with the outfit, she figured Kennedy hadn't even heard herself say that.

Hillary slipped out of her dress, right in the center of the room, and took the new dress off the hanger. Careful not to bother the small ties that were for store display, she unzipped the dress and stepped into it. She wiggled it up her body and then turned her back to Kennedy for her to zip it up.

Kennedy moved in behind her, took the zipper and stopped. "What size did you put on?"

"My size."

"These are running small. I can't get this zipper up."

Hillary winced. Those damn cinnamon rolls had taken their toll on her.

She adjusted her breasts, wincing at their soreness. "Don't keep trying. I'm PMSing. My boobs are swollen, my stomach is swollen, and I can't stop eating those cinnamon rolls from the bakery."

"I told you they were bad news."

"Give me the next size up. I promise myself, in front of you, I won't eat any more of them. They're the devil's food."

Kennedy laughed as Hillary slipped out of the dress. She readied the next size bigger and it fit, though Hillary thought it didn't look as nice as it should.

They accented the dress and Hillary spun herself around in the mirror.

"I really like this one. I hate this. I want to buy all the nice stuff you bring in."

"Sample sale only, darling. You know that."

"All too well."

The bells above the door chimed, and Kennedy poked her head out the door. "We're back here," she called out and Hillary assumed it was Joel coming back.

As she posed in front of the mirror, she looked to see Kennedy's father standing in the doorway with Chase and Max.

Did she look as bad as she felt? Yes, the dress looked nice, and they'd accented it as well, but it was a bigger size. Suddenly she felt completely self-conscious.

Mr. Devereaux whistled. "Hillary, you're a hot number."

Kennedy smacked her father on the arm. "Dad," she scolded in a hushed tone.

"Thank you, sir. This is a new acquisition from Paris."

"My girl does pick the nicest stuff." He pulled Kennedy in to his side, wrapping his arm around her shoulders. "Me and the boys are going to meet Paige next door. Do you have time for a drink? I know your husband keeps things there you can drink. I want to talk to you all."

Hillary kept her attention on the dress and the necklace they had added, trying to not listen.

"We'll close up in just a bit. I'll be over."

Her father kissed her atop the head before he and Max started out the door.

When Hillary looked back up, only Chase and Kennedy remained.

She turned to look at both of them.

"Aren't you going with your dad and brother?" Hillary directed the question at Chase, and Kennedy then looked at him as if she'd forgotten he was there.

"Couldn't help but admire the view," he said with a wink before he turned to leave.

CHAPTER 18

The tap house was buzzing, as it had since they'd opened it. Chase looked around the room. All of the tables were full, people mingled outside by the pizza truck, and others filled spaces and stood with a beer in their hand.

He hadn't done any of the work to get the business up and running, he'd only worked when they needed him, but he was filled with pride over the establishment.

Joel had blocked off a table for them and Paige already had a beer in front of her.

"Dad, what do you want?" Chase asked.

"Just get me what you like," he said.

Max nudged him away from the chair and then sat down. "Me too. Just get me what you like, brother."

Chase shook his head and headed back behind the bar. Amber was pulling beer now, and she smiled as he slid in with a tray and began to fill glasses. He pulled a sugar free, bottled lemonade out from the small refrigerator for Kennedy.

As he carried the tray to the table, Joel's brother Jeff caught his attention.

"Hey, I know you're not working. But I have a case of paper

towel in the back of my truck. Will you grab it and put it into storage? I have to change out the keg."

"Sure."

Chase delivered the drinks to the table and then headed out back to get the box from Jeff's truck.

That was when he saw Hillary opening the door to her car.

"You looked beautiful in that dress," he called out to her, but the sound of the music being played inside drowned out his voice.

She shook her head and started toward him. "What?"

As she neared him, he repeated, "I said you looked beautiful in that dress you had on. I mean it."

She laughed. "Little secret, it was a size bigger. I've become addicted to those cinnamon rolls at the bakery."

"I never would have noticed. You're not going to join us?"

Hillary narrowed her gaze on him. "Your dad needs to talk to you. You don't need me around, and I see that you don't have Tammi around either."

"Family night."

"Like I said, your father needs you. I'll talk to you later." She turned to walk away, but he caught her wrist.

"I miss you."

"You have seen me more in the past two months than you have in years. I can't imagine you're missing me."

"I miss not being awkward around you. I miss just being us."

She eased her arm from his hand. "That's what happens when friends sleep together. Hell, they write songs about it, and movies. We're okay. We'll be back to normal soon."

"I hope so."

"Have a good night," she called back as she walked toward her car.

He waited until she had pulled away before grabbing the case of paper towels and carrying it inside.

Chase set the box on the shelf in the storage room and then poured himself a beer before sitting down next to Paige.

His father looked at each of them and smiled. "I'm really proud of all four you. I didn't make anything easy on you, but you stick together and you're all fine adults."

Paige rested her hand on their father's. "Are you okay? I feel like you're giving some last inspirational speech."

He laughed a full robust laugh. "I'm fine. In fact, I'm great. I wanted to have you all with me. I have decided to move to Miami. I'm tired of snow."

Max leaned in. "Move to Miami? Like full up and move? You're not going to go check it out? You don't just want to vacation there? You want to move."

Their father leaned back in his chair. "That's what I said. Listen, I wasn't a stellar father, but I did my best. I'll be a good grandpa, but seriously, are you going to ask me to take care of the baby for a few years?" He directed his question to Kennedy who bit down on her lip. "Gloria has invited me to come stay with her. She lives in a nice trailer park for seniors. I think it'll be a fantastic change of pace for me."

Chase had never wrapped his head around the relationship his father was having with the woman he'd met on the cruise ship. She flew home with him after his heart attack and took care of him when they'd just met. How asinine was that?

Then again, he nearly lived with Tammi, who he'd known for a little over a month. Who was he to point fingers?

Kennedy slid her bottle around the space in front of her on the table. "What do her kids say?"

"Her kids are all grown up too. It doesn't matter what they say or what you all say. I'm moving to Miami."

Chase watched the faces of his siblings. He noted worry from Kennedy, anger from Max, and sadness from Paige. What did he feel? Did he care?

It wasn't that he had anything against his father, but the man should do what the man wanted to do. Or was that just what the bastard child would think?

He was surprised by his own thoughts. Chase loved the man, as did the other three sitting there. He'd stepped up and was as near as perfect a father as a man could be when he had nothing to do with the mother and was never married to her. But that wasn't because of Chase, and he knew it. His father had always been sure to make sure he understood that.

But he didn't care if he took off to live in the heat with some woman. Just like he didn't care that the dress was a bigger size on Hillary or that they were friends. If they wanted to have sex and keep having sex, then they should.

When Kennedy said his name, as if she'd said it more than once, he realized his thoughts had completely derailed.

"Sorry, what?"

"Do you still know the guy with the moving company?" she asked her question again.

"Oh, yeah. I'll give him a call. He can estimate the move for you fairly quickly."

His father gave him a warm smile of appreciation, and Chase drank down his beer hoping it would ward away the thoughts he was having of Hillary.

CHAPTER 19

While *You Were Sleeping* was on TV, and Hillary couldn't go without watching it. Sure, it was interrupted by commercial breaks and had been altered for TV, but she didn't care. She knew all the words and had all the cut scenes vivid in her mind. It was movies like this, the ones she cherished so much, that she could keep on for background noise and get things done around the house.

The moment she'd gotten home, she'd take her bra off since it was killing her. She slipped into a bubble bath, shaved her legs, and gave herself a facial.

While the mask hardened, she cleaned up her kitchen, in her pink robe and fuzzy slippers. Perhaps while she finished watching the movie, she'd give herself a mani/pedi too.

When the kitchen was tidy, she went back to the bathroom and opened the cupboard under the sink to search through her bucket of nail colors. OPI, Essie, Orly, she had them all. Red, pink, purple, black—she was obsessed. There was one bottle of *Kennedy Pink* also, Kennedy's signature nail color, but she just wasn't feeling pink tonight.

There was another bucket of colors toward the back.

She pulled out the toilet bowl cleaner and the extra toilet paper. Then she moved the tampons and maxi pads, only to stop and stare at them. She had bought a new box of tampons and a new bag of pads before Kennedy's wedding so that she was covered if her period came during the wedding. Nothing would have been worse than if it had come early and she was in the dress.

But it hadn't come, and she didn't think a thing about it.

Those packages had been unopened since she bought them in February, now it was the middle of April.

Hillary scrambled to her feet and pulled open the drawer to the cabinet, pulling out the calendar that she kept there. She scanned over all the markings in it and important dates.

She flipped through the pages, back to Kennedy's wedding, and then before that. Christmas brunch with her mother. Christmas Eve at her cousin's house. New Year's Day movie marathon. Fitted for maid-of-honor dress for Kennedy's wedding. Period, January thirtieth.

Sex with Chase Devereaux, February fifteenth.

Hillary's lip began to sweat beneath the hardened mask on her face as she pulled open the medicine cabinet and shuffled the bottles around. She picked up her birth control packet and opened it. When was the last time she had even taken one of these? She gave it some thought. She hadn't taken them to Mexico—heck, she hadn't taken them since she'd gone with Paige to a yoga retreat weekend and had forgotten to pack them.

She pressed her fingers to her trembling lips and then pressed her hands to her breasts. She'd been two months without a period.

The world around her began to spin and she sat down on the toilet and put her head between her knees. It would be normal to be worked up, she thought, if this in fact was a problem. There was no way she was pregnant. They'd used a condom.

They had used a condom, right?

Safe sex was top priority to her, how could she have missed a step? Easy, because she was with Chase, and it was easy to forget something when you realized you were in love with someone who wasn't right for you.

Then she sat up and thought of the dress Kennedy couldn't zip up. The cravings for cinnamon rolls. Her vacation in Mexico. And her mind replayed it all again, only this time she remembered the shower sex the next morning.

She reached for the calendar again and counted the weeks from the wedding to her vacation.

"Shit. Shit. Shit!" she yelled as she hurried out of the room to google morning sickness and when it comes about only to find that it all lined up.

Hillary sat down on the couch as Sandra Bullock's character Lucy told Jack's family what she'd done in her elaborate lie in the movie. But she didn't hear a thing, and it was her favorite part of the movie.

No, all she could do was think about the reality she was facing.

Tears began to roll down her cheeks and through the dry clay mask that was still on her face.

She needed to get a test, and now. Could she order one to be delivered in an hour? No, it wasn't DoorDash. She'd need to go and get a test. There was no time left to second guess what was going on.

Within a half hour, she'd washed off the clay mask, gotten dressed, and headed to Target to get a test. She would run in, self-checkout, and be home.

The store seemed more crowded than she thought is should be for eight o'clock on a Tuesday night. She hurried to the pharmacy and scanned the shelves of tests. One used the word pregnant, the other used a cup and a dip stick. Two pink lines, one pink line, mail in. Okay, she'd read that wrong, but she was out of sorts.

Opting for two different tests, she picked one that spelled it out and another that would show two pink lines—or one line when it was negative, and she was simply stressed out and eating too many cinnamon rolls.

Hillary held the boxes in her hands so that no one could read them, or so she hoped, and she walked toward the self-checkout. Walking up to the next open scanner, she scanned the items and dropped them into the bag quickly, and then pulled her wallet from her purse.

"Hillary?" someone said her name and she looked up to see a familiar woman at the scanner next to her. "Tammi. We only met once. Chase's girlfriend."

The world was spinning again, but Hillary sucked in a breath to stop it.

"Right. Hi."

"Chase was having a drink with his family, so I thought I'd do some retail therapy. You too?" she asked, glancing at the bag.

Hillary moved to shield the bag, just in case Tammi was looking to see what she bought. "Yeah. I ran out of toothbrushes for the guest bathroom."

"How is your hand doing?"

Hillary gripped hold of her bag after taking her receipt and felt the stitches brush against her fingers. "It's doing fine. Stitches come out tomorrow. It was nice to see you again."

"You too. Have a nice night," Tammi said as Hillary hurried from the store.

It wasn't even a full hour since Hillary had left her house in a rush until she was sitting on the toilet looking at the two sticks she had bought.

Her heart raced and sweat beaded on her brow as she watched two pink lines form and the word PREGNANT appeared in the window of the other stick.

CHAPTER 20

Chase opened the front door of his house and all the lights were on. Tammi stood at the stove stirring something in a pot. She'd asked for the key so she could cook him dinner, and though it should have been a welcome sight, it bothered him to have her in his space without him.

And, he decided as he hung his jacket on the hook by the door, that was petty.

"That smells good," he said as he walked toward the kitchen and pulled a beer from the refrigerator.

"My mom's special sauce. I don't have a lot of culinary skills, but this I can manage."

"Well, my mom doesn't cook. Five kids, and she could usually only cut up hot dogs and make mediocre mac and cheese out of a box."

"I thought you only had three siblings. Max, Kennedy, and Paige."

Chase sat down at the kitchen table and chuckled. Here she was in his house, stirring sauce, she'd been sleeping in his bed, and she knew nothing about him.

A month ago, that would have been okay. Now, he thought

there should be more to a relationship. But what did he know of those?

"Those are the siblings on my father's side."

"So, in all you have..." She quickly did the math. "Seven siblings?"

"Yep."

"How many are full blooded?"

"Not a one. I'm a lone bastard."

Tammi set the spoon down and moved to him. She sat in his lap and wrapped his arms around his neck. "You're anything but. I've seen you with your siblings on your father's side. They adore you. But I want to hear the story."

Wasn't he tired of repeating it? But what would it hurt? It seemed like Tammi was going to hang around a while longer.

She stood and returned to her stirring duties and he took a long pull from his beer.

"My dad had an affair with my mom. He was married to Kennedy and Max's mom at the time, and my mom was leaning toward a divorce from her first husband. Kennedy's mom was pregnant with her when my mom got pregnant with me, and the divorce my mom had been considering became reality. She decided to keep me, but she and my dad called it quits. He went back home to his wife and had Max, but then got divorced right after that. I suppose she thought she could forgive him, but it was just too hard. Eventually, my mom remarried and had two more kids, and got one more divorce. Anyway, the best thing my mother ever did was give me my father's last name. He messed up. I mean really messed up. It tore his family apart, and he never married my mom. But he was there for me always. I might have some trust issues because I see how he handled things, but he was there for me. He raised me and Max and Kennedy together. So, we're tight. They always had my back. My mom, she made it clear that my siblings and I, from her side, were basically three different families."

"That's sad."

"That was life."

"Where does Paige fit in here? You haven't mentioned her."

"Dad married Paige's mom when I was about eight. Paige came along a few years later. She was the wanted one. The child from a happy marriage."

"Do you begrudge her that?"

"Hell no. She was lucky. And, she was part of our mix from day one."

She sipped the sauce from the spoon to taste it. "But your dad isn't married to her mom anymore?"

Chase took another long pull from his beer. "Paige was about six when her mother was killed in a car accident."

Tammi dropped the spoon in the sauce and jumped back from the stove, her hand on her arm. "Shit!"

Chase moved to her and looked at her arm where the sauce had splashed out. He took the towel from the side of the sink, wet it, and pressed it to her arm. "Are you okay?"

"I'm fine. That just surprised me, I guess. About Paige's mom."

She was fully engaged in the story, he supposed.

Tammi pulled the spoon out of the sauce, rinsed it off, and went back to stirring it. "Your dad raised Paige?"

"Yep. Kennedy moved in with them when she was a little older, and I found it was a good opportunity to get out of my mom's house too. We were Paige's village I guess you could say."

"I think that's precious."

Chase sat back down and lifted his beer to his lips as Tammi set the spoon down and leaned against the counter.

"And where does Hillary play into all of this."

Chase lowered his bottle, nearly choking on the beer as he swallowed. "Hillary?"

"Yeah. You all have this relationship with her."

"She was Kennedy's best friend growing up. I guess we all just adopted her. She's everyone's friend."

"But she is protective of you."

He sipped his beer again. "Is she?"

"Yeah. When I come around, she gets all freaked out. Like when I went to Kennedy's store to buy the dress and she broke the vase. I told her we were going to that event at the Saint Pierre and she went pale. She said she'd gone with you a few years ago, and she warned me not to wear purple."

Chase wondered if he, too, were turning pale as the blood drained from his face. "The boss' wife wears purple."

"That's what she said. Then that whole deal with cutting her hand and you taking her to get stitches. And tonight, I saw her at Target. I think she might have been in her pajamas. Her hair was a mess on the top of her head. She still had remnants of a facial mask around her hairline. She had on flip flops, but they were two different colors."

Chase eased back in his chair. "I talked to her at the tap house. She seemed fine."

"Well, maybe she was drunk," Tammi chuckled as she turned the heat down on the stove. "We were in the self-checkout. She scanned her items, threw them in a bag, and then cinched up the bag as fast as she could when I said hello. As if she didn't want me to see what she bought. Oh, and then she told me she had to buy new toothbrushes for the guest bathroom."

Chase took a breath to speak, and then stopped. Tammi didn't need to know Hillary didn't have a guest bathroom.

"I guess it's a mystery," he said nonchalantly, even if he was curious himself as to what was going on with her.

Tammi turned to the oven and slid a baking sheet of bread inside.

Chase strained his neck to see what she was doing. "Garlic bread?"

"Yep. Rigatoni. Meatballs. Homemade sauce. Garlic bread. Salad. I'm trying to impress you."

He couldn't imagine why. "I'm impressed."

"Good. I wanted to talk to you about something."

His hand gripped the beer bottle tighter. "What's that."

"A vacation."

At least she didn't say she wanted to move in or get married. He might have to quickly hit the brakes on that. "Where are you thinking about going?"

"Vegas."

"There is nothing to see in Vegas but drunks."

"There's plenty to do. I've never spent much time on The Strip, but my friend Jennifer just got back. They went to shows and ate amazing food. She only lost twenty dollars because she said there was so much to do, she didn't have to gamble. But she'd never done slots, so why not."

"Vegas, huh? I haven't been there in a while. Maybe it's changed."

"Should we plan it?"

"We can look into it. Did Jennifer just go out for a weekend?"

Tammi tucked her lips between her teeth as if she had a big secret, and she moved toward him with the spoon, lifting it to his lips to taste the sauce.

"She went out with a friend. There were a few of them actually. Then the friend met up with this guy she knew from high school, and then ran off and got married at one of those little chapels. Isn't that romantic?" She eased the spoon to Chase's lips, and he licked the sauce off.

"Married?" His voice shook.

"Married." She turned back to the stove and poured the rigatoni into the pot of water that boiled. "I can't even imagine."

And neither could he.

CHAPTER 21

Cold and sterile wasn't Hillary's thing. Her heart raced and her hands shook as she sat on the table in the doctor's office, her back exposed through the gown and her ankles crossed to keep her knees together.

She'd told Kennedy she'd be late because she needed to get her stitches removed, which wasn't a lie. But now she sat there aware that the results that the doctor was about to give her were the same ones she'd gotten at home.

When the door opened, the middle-aged woman whom had been her doctor for years smiled up at her. "Congratulations. You are indeed pregnant."

The air in Hillary's lungs was harder to push in and out and the doctor must have noticed. She moved to her and helped ease her back in a reclined position.

"Not expected?" the doctor asked.

"I expected you to say it. I didn't expect you to have to."

"You didn't plan for this pregnancy?"

"Not in a million years."

The doctor pulled her stool next to the table and raised it so that they were nearly eye to eye. She sat down and placed a hand on Hillary's shoulder. "May I ask a few questions?"

Hillary nodded. "Of course."

"You were not forced into this? I mean the conception."

Hillary shook her head. "No. Oh, God, no. I know the father. I love the father. I just…" she didn't know what else to say. "I just might be too late… I don't know what for." Tears welled in her eyes and spilled over her cheeks.

The doctor turned and pulled a tissue from a box and handed it to her.

"Thank you." She dabbed her eyes. "The father and I are life-long friends. His sister is my best friend." The words fell as freely as the tears now. "We hooked up a few years ago and that was all it was. His sister freaked out a bit, so we just never did it again. Then, when his sister got married, we got drunk, and well—here I am eight weeks later."

The doctor smiled. "You plan to tell him?"

"Of course. I just don't know how. He's in a new relationship, and his own parental story is as mixed up as this one."

"We have counselors that can help you through this. They can help you get a grip on it. They can be there for both of you, so you can tell him. You're not alone."

Hillary let out a breath. "I'm not alone. No matter what I do, I know I'm not alone. But I'm scared out of my mind. Babies were never in my plans."

"Nature has its own plan. Would you like to see your baby?"

The tears returned and all she could do was nod.

"I'll go get the machine. You stay calm and breathe."

The doctor returned a few minutes later and by then Hillary had composed herself. This was a reality she hadn't planned on, and now she just had to decide how she was going to tell Chase— or what she was going to tell him.

The wand and the machine were explained to her. She was early enough that the wand was vaginal. She didn't care, all she wanted was to see who was up there, making her sick, dizzy, and so emotional. The tears were back and this time they were accompanied with laughter.

"Everything okay?" the doctor asked.

"Just a whole lot of things making sense now. "

"It's good to have answers. Okay, here we go."

She inserted the wand and the picture on the screen began to change. Nothing made sense to her. There was a bubble, and a bigger bubble, then two bubbles. Nothing resembled a baby until the doctor moved the wand one more time and clicked a few buttons on the machine.

"There we are," she said, and Hillary lifted her head.

The bubbles all now formed a little person, and the tears intensified. "I have never seen anything so beautiful in my whole life."

"Would you like to hear the heartbeat?"

Hillary nodded.

Again, the doctor pushed a few buttons on the screen and the room filled with a whooshing sound.

"That's it? That's the heartbeat?"

"Beautiful, isn't it?"

It was like her favorite song. "Can I record it?"

"Sure."

The doctor handed Hillary her phone and she recorded the sound. Then the doctor printed out a picture of the sonogram for Hillary to take with her.

"You and the baby look fantastic. Your hand looks good too. It was a good thing you got it stitched up as quickly as you did."

She thought about Chase taking her the urgent care. And, at least now she knew why the sight of blood had made her so queasy that day.

When Hillary walked out of the office, she was enlightened. Unprepared, but enlightened.

She wasn't ready to tell a soul, but considering she already couldn't fit things in her normal size, her secret wasn't going to be much of a secret for long.

Then she thought about Kennedy, and she wondered how this would make her feel. It was time for her to be the spotlight of everything. A wedding. A baby. It felt as if Hillary were swooping in to take that from her—and with Kennedy's brother of all people.

And then there was Chase. He was less ready to be a father than anyone she knew. No, this was going to be a disaster.

Maybe she could have the baby and not tell anyone who the father was.

No, she couldn't do that to the baby, not after knowing how Chase felt about how he was raised. This baby needed to be loved and both parents needed to be involved.

Well, she had until November to flesh out the plans. For now, this was her secret. And though it wouldn't be a secret for long, it was hers.

Eventually someone would figure it out and then she'd figure it out.

Pressing her hands to her belly, she felt a calm she never knew existed and a love that already went deeper than anything she'd ever felt.

CHAPTER 22

Kennedy stood at the counter, a large gift bag and her new mother-in-law and young niece standing in front of her.

"Oh, Hillary, look what they brought me. Is this the cutest thing you've ever seen?"

She held up an outfit in green. Obviously gender neutral.

"It's adorable."

"And look. It has little shoes," she said with a delighted sigh as she held them up.

June Kingsley beamed as brightly as Kennedy did. "We saw them at the mall, and sweet girl thought her cousin should have them."

"That is precious."

Kennedy put the outfit back in the bag. "What did the doctor say?"

Instantly, Hillary felt the blood drain from her face. "What would the doctor say?"

"About your hand."

Hillary expelled a breath and looked down at the mark on her hand. "Oh. It's good. She said it was good that I got it stitched up when I did."

"Chase to the rescue, huh?"

"Yeah. I'll get to those new shipments now." She turned toward June. "It was nice to see you."

"You as well," June said as Hillary passed her and headed toward the storage room.

She shut the door and leaned up against it, pressing her hands to her stomach. She thought the joy of carrying her baby would last more than a few hours, but the pain of knowing she would be stealing the joy away from Kennedy broke her heart.

Would she have anyone that saw something cute and wanted her baby to have it? Who did she have that would do that? Well, Kennedy would if it were a different time.

Hillary pressed her fingers to her lips to keep the sob inside that threatened to release.

"It's you and me kid. We have to figure this out."

CHASE LOOKED at himself in the mirror. He might dress in a monkey suit to appease his clients on a normal basis, but he never wore a tie.

Tammi stepped in front of him and undid the knot he'd mangled. "How is it you don't know how to tie a tie?"

"I do know how to tie a tie. I choose not to wear them, so I get a little rusty."

"One, two, up and through," she said as she made quick work of the tie before she placed a kiss on his lips. "I love this dress I bought from your sister. What do you think?"

She twirled in front of him.

"It's nice."

"Just nice? Not sexy or hot?"

He chuckled. "Okay, sexy and hot."

"What do they do at this party?"

Chase thought about it. He'd gone every year for four or five years. The first year he took Hillary, and hadn't she radiated in that purple dress?

"It's just a business dinner. They serve you something fancy. Open bar. They give awards to their employees, and there's a gift bag on your chair. I'm one of those people he invites because he can. I get a free dinner out of it and I can impress my dates."

She pursed her lips as she directed her attention to his tie again. "And you took Hillary once?"

And why would she bring her up again, he wondered? "First year they invited me. Last minute thing."

"I saw her today when I picked up the dress. Kennedy had it altered for me. She didn't look well."

"No? Maybe she's just tired or something."

Tammi placed her hands on his chest. "It looked like she'd been crying. Of course, why would she cry when she works in a place where she's surrounded by so many beautiful things?"

"What was she crying about?"

Tammi laughed and pushed back, looking at herself in the mirror. "How am I supposed to know? I went to your sister's store, picked up my dress. I tried it on. Come to think of it, Kennedy said Hillary had been feeling ill, and I think she was getting sick in the bathroom. Small business, huh? You still need your employees to show up when they're sick." Her eyes went wide as if she'd realized that she'd snidely made a comment about his sister—or that's how he'd taken it. "I'm sorry. I didn't mean…"

"I know. Let's get going. The sooner we get there and make our appearances the sooner we can leave. I have an early client in the morning."

Tammi looked at herself in the mirror one more time. "Early client. That means you'll want to stay at your house?"

Chase ran his tongue over his teeth. "Yeah. I'll bring you home so I don't bother you when I get up in the morning."

When he turned and walked away, he knew she understood that he had no intention of spending the night with her. He hadn't meant to fall into any kind of relationship with her, or anyone.

Tammi was a fine choice when it came to companions. She was nice, pretty, and successful in her own right. But she just didn't fit, not the way he wanted the woman he spent time with to fit.

His problem was, he compared every woman to Hillary, and he had for years. Even his prom dates had never measured up.

She was off the table and off limits, but he couldn't help but worry about her. She hadn't been the same since she'd gotten back from Mexico, when he'd carried her to bed because she was so sick. Panic began to settle in his chest. Was something wrong with her—more than food poisoning or jet lag? The few times he'd talked to her in the past month she wasn't herself. She'd cut her hand and nearly passed out, and that wasn't like her at all. Usually, she was the strong one that took control in a crisis. Did he bring it up with his sister? Wasn't she out of sorts too?

He picked up his jacket and swung it on as he made his decision. Maybe Kennedy had some insight.

CHAPTER 23

There was a small amount of guilt that plagued Chase when he woke up the next morning. He'd taken Tammi home after the party and then had driven around for an hour. He'd made three passes by Hillary's house, but never stopped.

One time all of the lights were on in the house. The next time there was the flicker of a TV coming from her bedroom. The third time the house was dark, and he knew she'd gone to bed. He certainly wouldn't stop then.

Around one in the morning, he crawled into his own bed, alone and grateful. Things with Tammi had gotten too serious, and he'd only meant for her to be a distraction for a night. He'd have to give that some thought.

The next morning, he drove his client to the airport, just as he told Tammi he was going to do. Then he headed to his father's house with a bag of bagels and two tall coffees.

"Sunday morning bagels with my son? To what do I owe the pleasure?" His father asked as he opened the door and Chase stepped through.

"Just needed some time with my old man."

His father patted him on the shoulder. "I'll try to find the old guy. For now, you're stuck with me," he teased as they walked through the house to the kitchen.

Chase set the bag and the coffees on the table and then took a seat. His father sat across from him.

"Already out driving people?"

Chase nodded as he pulled off his jacket and hung it on the back of the chair. "Yeah. Regular client needed a ride this morning."

"Things are going well?"

"They are," he said with pride. "I'll be able to pay Kennedy off within the year, I think. And, I know she thinks she's not going to get it back at all, so it'll be a nice surprise."

His father took a bagel and twisted it open. "You look troubled."

And that was why he had come to his father. He needed someone who could see that.

"I have a girlfriend."

His father lifted a brow. "Tammi?"

"Yeah."

"I know that."

"That's not the point. Five weeks with the same woman and I'm completely out of sorts."

"You didn't come to me for relationship advice, did you? You've always held my lack of knowledge in this department over my head."

And that was true, Chase thought as he took a bagel and twisted it open just as his father had. "I have held that over you. I probably have been quite a dick about it."

His father chuckled. "You've grown up a lot. The fact that you're using the term girlfriend proves that."

"Can't remember a time I've ever used it."

"Neither can I. I know you enjoy women, perhaps a bit too

much." Chase winced when his father said that. "But I know you also care for people."

Or one person, he thought. "I just don't know if I want to have a girlfriend. I mean, I don't know that Tammi is the one."

His father shrugged as he bit into this bagel. "What did you say, five weeks? Is that enough time to know?"

"You met Gloria on a cruise ship and now you're picking up and moving."

The smile that formed on his father's face said that he was happy with his decision. "There is a moment when you know something is just right."

And hadn't Chase felt that when he'd been with Hillary?

He took the lid off his coffee and blew the steam from the cup. "Hillary and I had a night together."

His father stopped chewing and swallowed hard. "Kennedy's Hillary?"

The classification of it made Chase laugh. "Yeah, Kennedy's Hillary."

"A night, huh?"

Chase leaned back in his chair. "We had a night a few years ago. Back then that was all it was. Kennedy wasn't too pleased either."

"I can't imagine she would be."

"But after that time, we were still friends. I mean, I didn't judge her. She didn't judge me. It happened and we went on."

"This time it's different?"

"Yes. I don't know why. Maybe it's because I was comfortable and happy when she was there."

"So why didn't you ask her to stay?"

"I did, sort of. I mean—" He stopped and sipped his coffee as he replayed the conversation in his head again. Or what he remembered of it from a month ago. "I guess we didn't really discuss it. But I was open to it. I told her I love her."

His father nodded slowly as if he were taking it all in. "But she knew you loved her because you're friends."

"Right."

Chase's father reached out and laid his hand on Chase's arm. "I think you need a few more conversations with Hillary."

"And what do I do with Tammi?"

"I'm still trying to wrap my head around you coming to me for advice."

"I thought you'd have a lifetime of insight."

His father laughed as he eased back in his chair. "Insight given by the sinner."

"Dad..."

He held up his hand to ward off any argument. "I can tell you that if you give your heart to a woman, either woman, be true to that woman. If you're done, then walk away, don't expect that they should understand and accept your shortcomings."

"Is that your way of saying you regret your choices in life?"

Running his tongue over his teeth, his father narrowed his gaze on Chase. "I hurt my wife immensely. I tore apart my family. But the hardest part about answering this is that if I hadn't done what I did, I wouldn't have you. You're one of my greatest achievements, son. Our family isn't conventional, but we are that. We are a family and we've always been tight. However, getting another opportunity at love, I'm very focused on not ruining it."

"Love? Is that what this is between you and Gloria? Love?"

His father shrugged. "It's new. It's nice. It's an adventure. But as long as I'm figuring it out, I'll be faithful and true to her. You just need to decide who your loyalty lies with."

Chase picked up his coffee and sipped as his father ate his bagel. His loyalty was always with Hillary, but he knew there was no future.

CHAPTER 24

Hillary looked at herself in the mirror in the bathroom at the store. A new wave of morning sickness had started that week, and she'd so far managed to keep knowledge of it away from Kennedy.

Kennedy had begun to show, and on her cute little figure, her belly had just popped. The fashion icon she was, the shoes got flatter, but the outfits still looked amazing.

On the other hand, Hillary maneuvered her clothes as much as she could to conceal the ten pounds she'd already gained. There had been some humor as to her helping Kennedy with her weight gain, and she allowed herself to laugh even though those stupid hormones made her want to cry.

It had been two weeks since she'd been to the doctor and had confirmed what she'd learned on the floor of her own bathroom. But the picture, that perfect picture she'd brought home, it kept her going.

She kept it in her purse, laminated, just so she could look at it when she was feeling down. A little bit of her, a little bit of Chase, a completely imperfect world—and that was okay.

Hillary hadn't seen him for weeks. Certainly, he'd gone on

with his life. She heard that Tammi had planned a nice vacation to Vegas for them. Wasn't that sweet? Chase, the man who would never settle down was in a relationship and planning vacations.

Hillary had pushed him away because he wasn't that kind of man. And then he ran out and picked up a girlfriend. A girlfriend was a permanent fixture. Tears threatened again, but she wouldn't do it. She wouldn't give Kennedy reason for alarm. Kennedy was a married woman embracing her pregnancy, and she deserved to be doted on.

Hillary wasn't an idiot. She knew she couldn't keep this hidden or secret for much longer. And, Chase would know. He deserved to know. There would be a time.

She fixed her makeup and hair, opting to wear it in a ponytail to keep it out of her face. Packing back up her purse, she looked at the picture of her peanut one more time.

All of her life she thought she was chasing love. Just to have someone to love would be monumental. Never in her wildest dreams would she have thought that the love of her life would be the life that she grew.

"It's all going to work out," she said in a whisper before tucking the photo back in her purse and walking out of the bathroom.

Immediately, she heard giggling coming from the break room, and when she'd peeked her head in there, Cara, who used to work with them, had brought in her infant twins and her daughter.

"Oh my God! Look at them," Hillary again nearly burst into tears. "I didn't know you'd had them."

Cara stood and hugged Hillary. "When you have a little one at home, and then this, you just are on autopilot. It wasn't like when Melody was born, and you guys had to hurry me to the hospital. Brian dropped her off at his mother's house and we took a nice drive to the hospital for a C-section because Tabitha was breech.

Not in danger," she confirmed, "but we knew what we were up against."

Kennedy pulled one of the babies out of their carrier. "Which one is this?"

"Danielle," Cara confirmed.

Kennedy held her to her chest and sighed. "Oh, she smells so nice."

Cara looked up at Hillary standing next to her. "You can hold Tabitha."

It then hit her. She didn't know the first thing about babies, other than holding them and passing them back to their mothers if they needed something. Panic rose up in her and she turned back to the bathroom and hurled again. This was a mistake. A big mistake. How in the hell was she going to care for a baby alone? And even if Chase did step up, what help would he be? He was less paternal than she was maternal.

The tap at the door set in more panic.

"Hillary," Cara's voice was soft. "Are you okay?"

Hillary pressed a damp paper towel to her lips. "I'm fine. Just fighting a little bug, I think. I probably shouldn't be around the babies."

As soon as she'd composed herself, she gathered her purse and excused herself for the day. Kennedy would be asking questions. She'd better figure out what she was going to say.

As she opened the door to her car, she noticed the couple walking into the tap house, arms wrapped around each other, and laughter bubbling between them. Chase and Tammi seemed as happy as they could be, she thought. Not only was Hillary keeping this huge secret, but if she ever told Chase about the baby, the happiness he had with Tammi would be marred and he'd forever blame her.

She slid into the car, put on her seatbelt and just sat there. How could this have gotten so out of hand?

~

CHASE HAD MISSED the buzz of the tap room the past few weeks. They kept him on call and he liked that. His limo service was in high season now with proms, graduations, and weddings. There wasn't much time to consider working a night at the tap house.

Tammi had heard there was a pizza truck there that night, and she had a hankering for pizza before she headed off to work the night shift at the hospital. Chase figured it sounded good enough. This was a rare night where he wasn't working. Tammi had been making vacation plans for Vegas, and he was still not sure he wanted to go.

Joel was behind the bar, and instead of greeting them with just a *hello* he came around the bar and hugged them. "Sight for sore eyes," he said laughing. "Soccer mom association is having a fundraiser. They're louder than college girls."

"Need help tonight?"

"You free?"

"I am."

"I'll let you know. You here for pizza?"

Tammi nodded. "I've heard good things about this truck."

Joel nodded. "It's one of our favorites. You guys get some pizza, I'll pull you some beers. I have a new one on tap. IPA."

Chase nodded. "Sounds good."

"Just one of those lemonades for me. I have to go to work."

Joel nodded, pouring Chase a beer and opening a bottle of lemonade for Tammi.

They ordered their food and took it to the bar to enjoy their beers and keep Joel company. After an hour, Tammi kissed him goodbye and headed to work.

"Things are going good with you guys?" Joel asked as he washed the glasses behind the bar.

"I suppose."

Joel chuckled. "You don't sound sold on that."

"I'm not a relationship guy. Never have been. I like my free-dom. I like a change of scenery, if you know what I mean. I'm freaking stuck on what happened between me and Hillary, and I can't get her out of my mind. All the while, I have Tammi plan-ning trips to Vegas."

"Vegas is fun."

"Right. I've had plenty of fun there. But when she talks about it, she adds in the story of a friend who hooked up with a child-hood friend and they ran off and got married. We're two months in, and is that what she's thinking? Does she think I'll get to Vegas and want to get married?"

"That's deep."

"Deep end deep. I have some unresolved issues I need to figure out. I need to get Hillary and your wedding night out of my system before I can commit to anyone else."

The chair on the other side of him moved and he watched as his pregnant sister climbed up into it, her eyes narrowed on him and her lips pursed.

"Hillary and my wedding night? What in the hell does that mean?"

CHAPTER 25

C hase could feel the hairs on the back of his neck stand up. Joel cowering away hadn't gone unnoticed.

He lifted his beer to his lips and took a long sip. He wasn't going into this with his sister without being a little bit drunk.

"I asked you a question," she said, and she inched in closer to him. "You and Hillary? Again? On my wedding night?"

"Thirty-six-freaking-years-old, Ken. Leave me the hell alone."

"I will not. Hillary is my dearest friend in the world and you're some playboy. After last time I asked you to stay away from her and you did this?"

"Last time was five years ago. I did stay away."

"So why did you do it again?"

He drank down the rest of his beer and turned to her. "Because we happen to be attracted to each other. Because we, too, are friends. Because we like to have nights with other people. And because I care for her, damnit."

"You care enough for her that you have a one-night stand with her again and then get into a relationship, which, by the way, I'm impressed you've held out this long without running."

Oh, this wasn't going to end well.

Chase picked up his glass and walked around the bar to get a new one and fill it. Thinking of his sister, he opened her a bottle of water and slid it to her.

As he sat back down, he thought about what she was saying. She was right. The relationship he was in wasn't the norm. And that, too, was something he was trying to figure out.

Kennedy sipped her water. "She hasn't said a word."

"Of course she hasn't. She didn't want to hurt you."

"Well, this hurts."

"It's been two and a half months. We let it go. I think you can too."

She shook her head. "I guess what I don't understand is if you care for each other, why do this one-night thing? Isn't it gross?"

Chase chuckled as he sipped his beer. No, there was nothing gross about it.

"Can we just forget it?"

Kennedy sat for a moment in thought and then shook her head. "No. We can't. How come Hillary isn't good enough for you?"

That got his temper up quickly. "What the hell does that mean? She's perfect. If anyone isn't good enough, it's me." He took a long drink. "Which is what I think she was trying to get across to me the morning after."

"What does that mean?"

Chase finished his beer and turned to his sister. "If anything, she's the one that turned me away. She doesn't trust that we can have more than one night. We're not that kind of people."

"Your track record shows it."

"You're right. It did. But when I was with her, that wasn't an issue. I don't want anything but her. I even told her I loved her and that got me nowhere."

Kennedy's eyes grew damp. "You told her you love her?"

"I do love her. And I always have. Yes, it's a friendly love, but yes, it's gotten deep inside me. I can't get over this and now I have Tammi wanting to go on vacation and get married."

His sister's eyes went wide and she sucked in a breath before taking a sip of her water. "You just unloaded a ton of shit on me."

"Yeah, well it's been bottled up inside."

Joel cautiously walked back around the bar and took Chase's glass, but they both saw the stare Kennedy burned through him.

"You didn't tell me about this," she said to Joel in a low growl.

Joel exchanged a cautious look with Chase. "I didn't, because like he said, it was nothing."

"And how long have you known?" she asked.

Joel wiped up the counter, obviously trying his hardest to act normal. "Since the wedding. We talked about it the next day."

"And you all held this from me?" Her damp eyes filled, and tears rolled down her cheeks. "You don't think I can handle this?"

Chase put his arm around her shoulders only to have her shrug him off. "You're proving our point, you know. You don't want to hear it. Your best friend and your brother aren't perfect. And, they can sin together, and isn't that a shame?"

"You told her you loved her, and you still walked away."

Chase bit the inside of his cheek. "It's not like I didn't go back and try to be a friend or get her to talk. Listen, this is her call. And now I guess it's all too late. I have Tammi," he said, and he heard the venom in it. "I have Tammi," he repeated in a softer tone.

Kennedy picked up her water and held it to her lips. "Well this does explain a lot."

"Like what?"

"Like why she's been so weird for the past few months and why you don't drop by as often," she scowled as she sipped her water. "And why you punched Max."

"He ran off and told you that?"

"Nope. I made him spill it, but at the time it wasn't out of the norm for you guys."

"Sadly, it's pretty normal," he chuckled. "What I would appreciate is if you don't say anything to her. She doesn't need this crap in her life. What good does it do to know I'm having myself a pity party."

"You're good at them. She might not be surprised."

"Geez, thanks."

"Maybe if she knew you felt the way you did…"

"Nope. Don't do that. We went two different ways to save face around you. Don't go playing matchmaker or try to mend shit."

Kennedy eased back in her seat. "When do you leave for Vegas?"

"As soon as Tammi gets off work in the morning."

"Are you going to marry her?"

The response in his head was quicker than the one that came to his lips. "I don't know."

"Are you sure that's what she wants to do while you're there?"

Chase rested his hand on his sister's. "She's a romantic. Doesn't eloping on vacation sound like something you'd want to do?"

"I guess I'm married and having a baby with a man I didn't know a year ago. And the whole world is right."

"See what I mean? I don't know what will happen. I don't know if that's what she really wants either. She might want a cheap buffet and a drag show for all I know. But some sunshine and a pool sound good to me."

"Take care of yourself. And I promise, I won't say a word to Hillary. I might not see her for a few days anyway."

"Why's that?"

"She went home sick."

"I think she caught something in Mexico," Chase said. "Seriously, she hasn't recovered from that. I think she got alcohol or food poising or something."

"That was almost two months ago." Kennedy sipped her water and then her eyes grew wide.

"Are you okay?" Chase rested his hand on her arm. "You just went pale."

"I'm good." She looked him in the eye. "I'm good," she repeated and smiled. "Where did my husband go?"

"I think he's bussing tables."

"I have to go. Tell him I'll be home when he gets there." She hopped off the stool and kissed her brother on the cheek. "Hey, don't do anything stupid, okay?"

"What's stupid?"

"Marrying someone when you love someone else."

Was she grinning?

"I'll take your warning into consideration."

She kissed his cheek again and hurried out of the tap house as if she'd forgotten a date.

"Where is she off to?" Joel asked as he rounded the bar.

"I have no idea. I've seen that look before. She's got some wild idea and now she's run off to make it happen."

Joel smiled and set the glasses he carried next to the sink. "She does that in the middle of the night and then gets up and designs some piece of jewelry. Which, she sells the next day for three times the price of what she's got in it."

Chase looked at the door his sister had fled through. She was a wonder.

CHAPTER 26

Hillary sat at the kitchen table with a facial mask on, one of those out of the package ones that looked like a serial killer's mask. Her day had taken a turn for the worse as she'd left work. First of all, she didn't feel well. Second, she was embarrassed. Then she saw Chase and Tammi, which put her in even a worse mood, and then she'd gotten a parking ticket when she'd gone into the pharmacy to get prenatal vitamins. Luckily, while she'd been in there, she'd also bought some Rocky Road ice cream, which she was now indulging in after a nice bath.

She'd come to the conclusion that nothing was going to get better, so she might as well suck it up. She was, essentially, a single mother about to have her world rocked.

You've Got Mail was on TV, and it ranked right up there with *While You Were Sleeping* in her list of romances that she loved to watch and knew by heart. And though both romantic, she could see the fiction in the plot and therefore couldn't care that happily ever after wasn't real. It occupied her mind when she'd otherwise be sitting in a corner crying.

Just as she lifted her spoon to her lips the doorbell rang and then the incessant pounding followed.

"Hillary! I know you're in there. All of your lights are on and I can hear the TV. Tom Hanks would want you to answer the door!"

Panic set in when she realized it was Kennedy. She tossed down the spoon, hearing it bounce off the table and onto the floor as she ran to the door.

She pulled open the front door. "What's wrong. Get in here. Are you okay?"

Kennedy walked past her and straight to the kitchen. Hillary looked at the clock. It was eight o'clock. What on earth could have happened.

"You're freaking me out," Hillary said as she picked up the spoon, aware that it was already getting harder to bend over with a taut stomach.

"Having a spa night?" Kennedy asked looking at her with wild eyes and her arms folded in front of her.

"Yes." Hillary put the spoon in the sink and retrieved two more from the drawer. "I have more mask sheets if you'd like to join in. These don't leave residue in my hair," she said thinking of the last time she'd done a mask and run into Tammi at Target.

"Are you just going to go on like nothing happened?"

Hillary eased back down at the table and pulled the ice cream in closer to her. She slid the other spoon across the table, still hesitant to talk to the maniac that was Kennedy.

Was this a side effect of pregnancy? Was she going to start screaming at people too?

Hillary scooped out a spoonful of ice cream, and eased the spoon through the small hole in the mask. Contemplating her answer to the crazy question, she watched as Kennedy sat down across from her, took the spoon, and then reached for the tub of ice cream.

Hillary paused before handing it over.

"What are you really doing here? Why are you not home with your husband?"

"He's working and I'm worked up."

Hillary nodded. That much she'd gathered. "I see that. I'm not sure how I can help you."

Kennedy set the ice cream in the center of the table. "Chase," was all she said, and Hillary kept a steady eye on her. Already she didn't like where this was going.

"Good guy. Headed on vacation with his new woman. Is that what has you all bent out of shape? Afraid he'll gamble away what he owes you for his car?"

She wasn't humored, Hillary noted.

"You're going to make me do this?"

"Do what, Ken? You're starting to irritate me, and my ice cream is melting."

"I know you slept with Chase after my wedding."

The words had come out in a rush and Hillary was sure that she'd held her breath.

Slowly, she pulled the mask from her face, and wadded it up. "Well, that took a while for you to find out. Who ratted me out? Your husband? Max?"

"Everyone but me was in on this?" Kennedy pulled back the ice cream and dug in. "I'm not some child who has to be coddled."

"No, but you made sure to let us all know how you feel about this."

"Right," she said wincing from an apparent brain freeze. "Because when my best friend and my brother have sex, there runs the risk that they'll never talk to each other again. What if something happens and you two hate each other? I'm in the middle loving two people who can't be in the same room."

"That's not the case. Chase and I are fine. We decided to move on."

"He said *you* decided to move on. He said he told you he loved you."

127

Hillary eased back in her chair. "So, Chase is the one that told you we had a night together?"

Kennedy set the spoon in the center of the ice cream tub. "He was talking to Joel. I came in on that part. I don't think he wants to go with Tammi on this Vegas trip. I think he's afraid."

"Afraid of what? And I'm sorry, he told you he said he loved me?"

"Yes." Kennedy moved her chair around to the side of the table nearer to Hillary. "I'm pissed that you kept this from me."

"It wasn't any of your business."

"I'm pissed because you two should be together and because you're tiptoeing around me, you're both miserable."

"I'm not miserable," Hillary defended as she took the ice cream tub and scooped out another spoonful. "I'm just fine. I've always been just fine."

Hillary watched the expression on Kennedy's face change. She didn't believe her when she said she was just fine. They knew each other well enough, that often Hillary knew what she was thinking.

"Tell me about Mexico."

That wasn't what she'd expected her to say. "Mexico was nice. I sat on the beach and drank margaritas."

"With who?"

"No one."

"You're lying. Who took all the pictures?"

This time Hillary stood, taking the ice cream with her and putting it back in the freezer. She was done sharing.

"You want to know the truth? Some woman in the cabana next to me took all those pictures and I put them online so it looked like I was having one hell of a time. Truth was, the moment I got there, I wasn't feeling well. I had a half of that margarita in the pictures and then spent the rest of the week in my room. Happy? I didn't have one ounce of fun in Mexico."

"And then you came home and let Chase take care of you."

"Let him? I didn't have a choice. He was there when I got off the airplane. I didn't ask him to be there. Besides, if I remember right, he called you and you came."

"And why were you sick?"

"People get sick, Ken."

"Are you going there? Are you going to make me do this too?"

"Do what?" Their voices were rising, and Kennedy stood up and met her eye to eye.

"Are you pregnant with Chase's baby?"

CHAPTER 27

Hillary's hands shook, and the world began to spin. Had Kennedy just said that?

There was a part of her that wanted to attack back. How dare she stand there and accuse her of—but it was true. It was all true.

"You don't know what you're asking."

Kennedy shook her head. "Don't do that to me. I know exactly what I'm asking. Hill, look at me." She opened her arms to draw attention to her body. "I know what the hell it looks like to be pregnant and feel like crap. The only difference is that I'm being showered for it. Tell me it's not true and I'll leave right now, and we'll let this go. Just between you and me." She stepped forward and took Hillary's shaking hand in hers.

"Hillary, I'm not accusing you of doing anything wrong. What I'm asking is, are you carrying my niece or nephew?"

Hillary focused on her breath as it was becoming harder to breathe. She turned toward the counter and opened her purse. She pulled the coveted photo and handed it to Kennedy.

"Ten weeks now. That was taken at eight."

Tears began to roll down Kennedy's cheeks. "You're having a baby."

"I am."

Kennedy took the picture and sat down at the table.

Still hesitant, Hillary waited a moment before she joined her. She wasn't sure what Kennedy was processing, but it didn't seem as if she were mad.

Kennedy lifted her eyes from the photo. "You've been doing this for ten weeks all by yourself."

"I haven't been doing much."

"No, you've done a lot. It has to have been exhausting side-stepping everyone."

"There's a lot at stake, Ken. I couldn't lose you over this. And Chase, well, he's got other things going on."

Kennedy reached her hand out and clasped Hillary's in hers. "He would change any plans he has for you. He loves you."

"Like a sister."

"And that statement is gross," she laughed, and Hillary did the same. "I don't think that's how he loves you at all."

"He's a player."

"You were a player. I would assume your thoughts are else-where now."

Hillary took the photo from Kennedy. "This is the only thing that matters now. I don't know how I'm going to do this. I mean, how am I going to take care of a baby and work? How am I going to do this alone?"

"You'll never be alone, Hill. Max is starting the nursery in the store next week. We'll just have a new groove. Oh, hell, what did Cara put in the water there?" She laughed again as she pulled Hillary into her arms and held her there. "I love you, Hill. I'm so sorry you thought you had to hide this from me. Chase is going to want to know and he's going to want to be involved."

Hillary eased back. "I know, but he's with Tammi and that's a shitty thing for me to do to her."

"It's new. I don't think he loves her. Not like he loves you."

"You keep saying that."

"Because I mean it. You didn't see his eyes when we were talking. God, I feel so guilty."

"Don't. I should have told you. I should have told him. Hell, it's just been so confusing, and I can't believe you figured it out."

"I'm smarter than you think I am."

Hillary shook her head. "You're the smartest person I know. Okay, I guess I have a few days to work on what I'm going to tell him. How I'm going to tell him."

"I'm here for you. Take all the time you need. Days off—whatever. And no matter what happens between you and Chase, I'm thrilled that you're having his baby and we're going through this together. I can't think of anyone better to have as my sister."

"I love you, Ken."

"I love you too. Now, if you haven't eaten dinner, can we make something better than ice cream? I'm starving and you need to take better care of yourself."

Hillary pulled Kennedy to her again and held her. Why had she been worried? This was exactly what she should have expected from her best friend.

CHAPTER 28

The lights of the Vegas strip twinkled outside the window in the early morning. On any other trip to Vegas, Chase would have missed the sight because he'd have been hungover. And though they'd partied hard enough last night, there was some solace in knowing whose arm was draped over him and that he was in his own hotel room.

"What are you thinking?" Tammi's voice was soft in his ear.

"Just taking in the sight outside."

"I love Vegas. I know that to some it's just some party town or some pitstop along the way, but beyond this street there are lives that unfold."

"That sounds like experience talking."

She hummed. "UNLV School of Nursing," she said with some pride. "Worked at the hospital my first year and then moved somewhere I didn't just have drunk tourists throwing up on me. Like I said when I brought up this trip, I never spent much time on The Strip."

He chuckled slightly as sleep was beginning to take over his body.

Tammi traced her finger over the tattoo on his shoulder. "The only time I asked about this tattoo you said you got it with a friend."

"Yep."

"What kind a friend wants a guy to get a watercolor butterfly?"

"The kind of friend who likes butterflies."

"A woman friend?"

He would be honest, and he assumed it would get ugly, but he had to feel out the waters.

"Yes, a woman friend."

"Hillary?"

That hadn't taken long. "Yes, Hillary."

"I haven't seen you around her a lot. Well, I guess really just the day you took her to get the stitches and then when I picked up my dress, but she didn't say much to me. But she must be a very special friend to share this with you."

"I've known Hillary most of my life. She ran with Kennedy since junior high at least. So, yes. She's a very special friend."

"So how did this come to be?"

Chase laid there still trying to decide what she needed to know. "We got drunk after that fancy dinner. The one I took you to this year. She'd worn a purple dress, and the chatter was comical that she'd done it to scorn the owner's wife. We had some fun with it and drank too much. Somehow, we thought getting tattoos was a good idea after the party."

"And she talked you into this one?"

As he recalled she could have talked him into almost anything, and yet, neither of them had mentioned going to bed together, but they had.

"Yeah. She fell in love with it and a man plied with enough alcohol will do almost anything for a pretty girl."

"You never dated?"

And there was a solid answer to her question without lying. "No. We never dated."

"She's a party girl?"

He thought about it. "She likes a good time, but she's not a club girl or a stay out all night kind of girl. If that's what you mean? Why are we talking about her?"

"Just getting to know you more and I knew the tattoo had a story." She kissed his ear. "Do you think something happened to her in Mexico?"

Chase kept his eyes on the blinking lights of the MGM sign. Talking about Hillary was about the last thing he wanted to do right now, but Tammi had questions, he might as well answer them.

"Yes. I do think something happened to her. I think she got sick. I don't know if it was the food or the alcohol, or if someone drugged her. But she hasn't been herself since then."

Tammi let out a hum and kissed his shoulder blade. "I was thinking something else. It would explain why she got sick or has been sick."

Still not sure why Tammi was worried about it, he took a deep breath. "What do you think happened to her?"

"I think she hooked up with someone and got pregnant."

Chase flipped to his other side to face her, causing Tammi to jump back, eyes wide. "I beg your pardon."

"I think she's pregnant."

"You heard this? She told you this?"

"Why are you getting so defensive? It's not like you were in Mexico with her. I think you were with me."

He rested his hand on her shoulder and took another breath. "I worry about her. Like a sister," he said but then could taste the vileness of the words the moment he used them. "What makes you think she's pregnant?"

"Because I'm a nurse and I know what it looks like. I'm probably talking out of line," she said smiling and easing toward him.

"Seriously, tell me."

A crease formed between her brows. "That day I went to buy

the dress, she looked sick, but c'mon, I'm trained. I know when you have the flu or there's something else wrong with you. And," she began as she slipped her arm around him, "that night at Target, I saw what she had in that bag. She was trying to hide it, but she had two different pregnancy tests."

There was a pain in Chase's chest that had him gritting his teeth. "Why didn't you tell me that?"

"Wasn't my business."

He bit down on his lip. Hillary had gone to Mexico and come back pregnant. The very thought sickened him, and yet, it shouldn't have. He was in Vegas wrapped in the arms of someone other than Hillary. It was only fair that she'd gone to Mexico and done the same thing.

Tammi pressed a kiss to Chase's chest and then rolled until she straddled him. "New topic."

Thank God, he thought.

"You know, we've been together for months."

"We have," and hadn't he contemplated what kind of record that was multiple times in his head?

"I'm not getting any younger. And neither are you. I'm already forty and you're right behind me. We're both successful adults who have our shit together."

He wanted to laugh, because there hadn't been a time in his entire life that he'd felt like that.

"Thanks for the faith," he interjected, and she smiled down at him.

"Chase, I'm being serious. I have something to ask you."

He swallowed hard, keeping his eyes locked with hers. "What?"

"Chase Devereaux, will you marry me? Here in Vegas?"

That ache in his chest was back. He'd known all along this was her plan. He'd even mentioned it to Kennedy.

What was he supposed to do?

If what she said was true, Hillary didn't have time for him

anymore, not that she had. She'd dismissed him. They'd decided that they couldn't be something and that was why he had a naked woman atop of him asking him to marry her. He had to keep that in perspective.

"You're sure you want to marry me?"

"More than anything." She smiled down at him. "So? Will you marry me?"

He took one more breath and weighed his options in his head.

"Yes. Yes, I will marry you."

CHAPTER 29

Chase wasn't sure Tammi had gotten any sleep. The moment he said he'd marry her, she was on a quest. She'd armed herself with some basic knowledge of the wedding industry in Las Vegas, but there was so much more.

Each hotel had their own chapel, and each was better than the first one they looked at. But there was still the draw of the Little White Chapel at the other end of the strip.

And as far as Chase was concerned, they all looked alike.

Though it would be a quick ceremony, with only the two of them in attendance, she still wanted a wedding dress. There would be pictures, and those would be forever, so she wanted the whole package.

Watching her flit from store to store should have brought Chase immense joy, but he still wasn't sure what the hell he was doing. He'd been in a fog since Tammi had mentioned that Hillary had bought pregnancy tests.

As Tammi came out of yet another dressing room in yet another dress, he thought of the day he'd walked into Kennedy's store with his father and brother, and Hillary was in that stunning dress. And later, hadn't she admitted it was a different size than normal?

Tammi returned to the dressing room and Chase rested his face in his hands. He supposed there would be a lot to talk about when he got home.

AFTER THREE HOURS, Tammi had settled on a dress that she would rent. They had reserved the chapel at the Bellagio for the next morning, because there'd been a cancelation. Since there wouldn't be a reception, they upgraded their room to the honeymoon suite and ordered a dinner that would be delivered on their wedding night, which included a small wedding cake.

Since the sun was still high in the sky, they spent the rest of the day at the pool. Tammi had wanted the perfect honeymoon, so they agreed to take no phone, tablets, or computers with them while they lounged in the sun.

As they sat there, the sun beating down on them, a server brought over a tray with a bottle of champagne and two glasses. "This is compliments of the hotel as our way of saying congratulations on your wedding tomorrow."

Tammi reached up and took the glasses and bottle and set them on the table between them. "Oh, that was very kind. Thank you so much."

As the server walked away, Tammi poured them each a glass.

"Wasn't that nice."

"Very nice," Chase said taking the glass and sipping before he noticed the look on Tammi's face.

"We need to toast."

"Right." He held up his glass and waited.

"To us, and brand new beginnings."

"To us." He tapped his glass to hers and then drank down the contents of the glass hoping for the slightest buzz to carry him through the rest of the day.

"We haven't discussed where we'll live," she said as she sat back in her lounge.

"We haven't discussed a lot of things." His words now had a snap, and he assumed that was compliments of his buzz.

When he shifted his glance toward Tammi, he saw that it had sounded as harsh as he'd thought by the expression on her face.

He reached for her hand. "We have plenty of time to discuss living arrangements and everything else."

Everything else, he thought again, such as having a family or staying in the same town. Hell, she'd met his father, but she hadn't met his mother. And he hadn't met hers. And her incessant issues with Hillary—or what he thought were issues—were those going to be a problem?

And then again—what did it matter? He was inching toward forty and he had no better options. When he thought of it that way, he hated himself for it. Tammi wasn't a burden. It was his own fault that he'd climbed into the back of that limo with her, and the rest was history. The companionship had been nice for the past few months. It had been time for Chase Devereaux to grow up and have a relationship.

When they left the pool, they went back to the room and readied for dinner. Chase had made reservations at the steak house and acquired a table out by the fountains so that they could see the performance while they ate.

"It's crazy to think that by this time tomorrow we'll be married," Tammi said as she picked at her salad.

"You're sure you want to marry me?"

She set her fork down. "It sounds like you're having second thoughts."

"No," he said shaking his head. "I just never thought about myself as a catch for anyone. I guess I've just always thought of myself as a misfit."

She covered his hand with hers. "Anything but. I am so excited to be your wife."

And that was what he'd wanted—needed—to hear.

"I got you something," he said as he pulled a Tiffany blue box from the pocket of his jacket.

"What is this?" she asked removing the bow.

"We can pick out real rings later, when we know what we really want. But I thought this would look nice with your dress."

She pulled the Tiffany Heart Bracelet from the box and her eyes filled with tears.

"Chase, this is beautiful."

"I'm glad you like it." He took it from her and clasped it on her wrist. "You deserve something nice."

As the fountains began to dance before them, Tammi leaned in and kissed him.

THE NEXT MORNING, room service arrived with breakfast and shortly after that, the items they had rented for the wedding. The florist would meet them at the chapel with the flowers.

When Tammi opened the bathroom door and stepped out in her wedding dress, Chase's heart did a little dance. She was beautiful. This day was for her and he wanted it to be perfect. He couldn't promise her perfect once they got home, so one day, he could give that to her.

"You look amazing," he said standing and walking toward her.

"So do you. You always look so spiffy in a suit."

"Are you nervous?"

"Yes. You?"

He shook his head and kissed her cheek. "No. Let's go do this."

CHAPTER 30

Hillary sat on her sofa, feet perched on the coffee table, a bowl of yogurt rested on her belly. Now that Kennedy knew about the baby, and had warned her to take care of herself, she decided she would try. But having ice cream was so much nicer, she thought.

Tonight's movie du jour was *When Harry Met Sally*. She could go for the classic tale of friends to lovers as it would take her mind off everything, or so she'd hoped.

Just as Sally rolled over in bed with a wide-eyed Harry, Hillary's doorbell rang and then the incessant knocking started.

She shook her head, set down her bowl, and walked to the door. "Kennedy, you can call first. You don't have make such an entrance," she called out as she pulled open the door.

Standing before her, with a bouquet of roses, wasn't Kennedy at all.

"Max, what are you doing here?"

"Listen, I talked to Kennedy. Now, don't get mad at her, I kinda guessed what was going on. But she told me what's been going on with you."

There was a sense of betrayal that zipped through her,

but she knew better than to be annoyed by Max standing before her. If ever there was a good guy in a situation, it was him.

"I don't want anyone's sympathy. I'm fine."

Max stepped inside and closed the door. "I'm not giving you sympathy. I'm giving you support." He handed her the flowers.

Hillary took the bouquet and walked back to the kitchen with them as Max followed. "I appreciate it. I really do."

"Kennedy called me to her store this morning to go over some new details for the remodel. She's keeping you in mind. You and your baby, that is."

"She's the most amazing friend I have ever had. Sister—" she reconsidered. "She's an incredible sister."

Max pulled out a chair at the table and sat down. "If you need anything done here, you let me know. I'm happy to do whatever you need. As a brotherly favor."

Hillary turned, the flowers now shoved into a water glass, and she set them on the table before joining Max.

"I did get lucky when I fell into the Devereaux clan," she said smiling.

Max reached across the table and took her hand. "We're a mixed can of nuts. You fit in just fine."

That made her laugh, and didn't that feel good? But the mood grew serious as Max covered the hand he was holding with his other hand.

"Have you told him yet?"

Hillary shook her head. "I'm going to. As soon as he gets back from Vegas." She watched him flinch. "What's wrong?"

"Nothing."

Hillary pulled her hands back. "You have something to say. You know something. What?"

"It's nothing. It doesn't matter right? Things are good. You're taken care of. I'm here for you, Hill. No matter what you need —ever."

"Max Devereaux, if you don't tell me what you're talking about, I'm going to..."

"Don't hit me. Chase already did that."

She eased back. "What?"

"When he took in after me the night I walked into the tap house with you and had my arm around you. Remember? He took me out back, punched me in the face, and I knocked him on his ass, getting in a few licks."

She did remember they'd discussed it. "I can't believe you got into a fight over me."

"Hey, if I were going to go down defending the honor of a woman, it might as well be you."

"I don't understand."

"What's not to understand? He loves you and he's the biggest freaking idiot because he took your rejection to heart. You told him that you couldn't be together, so you're not. He's in Vegas and by now, he's probably married."

She felt the blood rush from her head, and she placed her head in her hands to hold herself steady. "Did you say he's probably married?"

"Shit, Hill. I didn't mean to blurt it out like that."

"He went to Vegas to get married?"

"No, he went to Vegas on vacation, but he knew she wanted to get married."

"So this is all just assumption?"

He paused, drew in a breath, and shook his head. "No. He called Kennedy to tell her. But none of us knew what to tell you."

She flew from her seat, and then balanced herself by holding onto the counter. "You drew the short straw? You got the unlucky job of telling the woman who is carrying his baby that he just married someone he's known for less than three months?"

Max rose. "Hillary, don't get so worked up."

"Worked up?" Her voice rose. "Who's worked up?"

Well, she thought, she was. She pressed her hand to her chest

147

because her heart rate had kicked up so fast, she worried it might explode.

"Settle down. This isn't good for you or the baby." He took her by the shoulders and set her back in the chair, just as there was another knock at the door.

Max watched her as he went to the door and opened it. Kennedy pushed past him and straight to Hillary. "You told her. Damnit, you told her."

"I thought that was the plan," he argued. "She needed to know, and you said it would be best coming from me."

"At least you brought her flowers," she huffed and gave him a shove.

Hillary looked up at Kennedy who had taken the seat next to her and gripped hold of her hands. "Are you okay?"

"He got married?"

Kennedy nodded. "He texted us a picture this morning before the ceremony. But that was all he said and then he must have turned off his phone. None of our texts were read."

"Married."

Kennedy turned to Max. "Get her some water."

Max opened the refrigerator and pulled out one of the bottles of sparkling water she kept in there. He twisted off the top and handed it to her.

"Sip," Kennedy instructed, and Hillary obliged. "He will be here for you and the baby. You know that as well as I do. He's already missed out on three months of your pregnancy, so you have to give him a chance to be part of it."

"I don't have to do anything," she argued.

"Yeah, but is that really what you're thinking?"

She didn't know what she was thinking. Every part of her had gone numb, including her brain.

CHAPTER 31

Max stood off to the side, his arms crossed over his chest. Hillary looked up at his calm and sweet eyes. She probably scared him to death with her antics.

She rose and walked to him. Wrapping her arms around his neck she squeezed him to her until his arms came around her.

"I'm sorry you had to be the bearer of bad news. Or of the news. I guess for Chase it's not bad news."

He eased her back to look at her. "You needed to know. But he's going to be miserable. I can guarantee it, and I'll relish it." He smiled. "When he knows what he's done, he'll never forgive himself."

"I don't want that for him either. This baby will be loved by both of us, by all of us, and we'll give him or her the best life we can. Your father did that for him, and I know he realizes that out of an unfortunate situation your father made the best of it."

He nodded and pressed a kiss to her cheek as there was another thunderous knock on the door.

Hillary laughed. "I get more noisy visitors after eight o'clock," she said.

"I'll get it." Max walked away and opened the door.

In one swift move he was pushed up against the wall and both Hillary and Kennedy screamed as Chase drew back his fist.

"You couldn't wait to sweep in, huh? Damsel in distress needs a hero?" Chase growled through gritted teeth.

Max lifted his hands to Chase's chest and shoved him until he had Chase pinned against the adjacent wall. "Why don't you pull your head out of your ass and stop accusing me."

"Both of you knock it off," Kennedy yelled as she came between them, pushing them apart. "What in the hell has gotten into you?"

Chase kept his eyes on Max. "She doesn't need his saving."

"I came as a friend, you asshole." He moved forward and Chase flinched, but Kennedy kept them apart.

Chase turned to Hillary. "I'm sorry. I'm sorry I busted in here. I suppose you're taken care of. I'm sure Max promised you the world."

Hillary crossed her arms in front of her. "You are a crazy man. I don't even know what you're talking about. And where's your wife?" She spat out the words, planting her fists firmly on her hips.

"I don't have a wife."

"Bullshit. What do you think they're here for? To tell me you got married this morning."

He shook his head and walked toward her. "I'm going to assume that Tammi is at the pool drinking away her pain with her best friend, whom I called and paid for her flight to go be with her."

"You left her there on your wedding day?"

He took Hillary's hands in his. "I didn't get married, Hill. I couldn't do it. Not after what Tammi told me about you."

Hillary's mouth went dry. "What did she tell you?"

"She thought you were hiding something about Mexico. And when she saw you at Target that night, she knew you'd bought pregnancy tests."

Hillary lifted her fingers to her mouth to hold back the sobs.

Chase moved her to the chair and sat her down, kneeling in front of her. "She told me she knew you were pregnant, and now that I look at you," he said scanning a look over her, "I see it. I don't know how I missed it."

"Chase..."

"Listen, I know that you probably don't know who the father is—just someone you met in Mexico, but I couldn't get it out of my head. I should be here for you and not marrying someone I don't even know."

Max moved across the room, grabbing Chase by the back of the shirt and yanking him back up to his feet.

"You know, I should throw the first punch. You are the most incredible, insensitive asshole on this planet. Apologize to her right now."

Chase shifted a glance to Hillary and back to Max. "What the hell did I say?"

"You jackass, you're the father of her baby. You!"

Chase turned his head to look at her. "Me? This is my baby?"

The tears had begun to roll down Hillary's cheeks as she nodded.

Chase pushed Max back and ran his fingers through his hair. "Me?"

"Yes, you. It happened the night of Kennedy's wedding."

He ran his hand over his face and thought about the lack of condoms in the trash that next morning. "You weren't protected?"

Hillary pursed her lips. "I guess I forgot."

"Wow, this is a lot."

"Well, I don't expect anything from you. I knew you'd react like this. Funny, you were more heroic coming in thinking I was just knocked up."

"You don't know anything about how I feel."

"You're right. Maybe you should just go, and I'll let you know when the baby is born."

Chase stood there a moment before passing by his brother and sister and heading out the door.

~

WHEN CHASE'S father opened the front door, he didn't say a word. He pulled Chase into his arms and held him. There was the same comfort as when he was little and had fallen off his bike.

"C'mon," he said pulling him into the house. "I have some coffee on. Let's talk."

Chase sat down at his father's kitchen table and watched as he took the whiskey out of a moving box and poured a shot into each of their mugs before bringing them to the table.

"Looks like you could use a little something stronger than just coffee tonight."

Chase wrapped his hands around the mug. "Thanks. I see you're all packed up. Time got away from me. I should have been here helping you more."

"You're living your own life," his father said. "I'll have a list of things for you to help me with when you come to visit me in Florida." He sipped his coffee. "So, what happened? You're not in Vegas with your new bride."

Leaning his elbows on the table, Chase lifted his mug with both hands and took a sip. "I left her at the altar. Well, at the door before we walked in. I just couldn't do it. I don't know her."

His father rested his hand on his arm. "Better to have done it then than to have led her through a life she didn't want—or you didn't want."

"I'm in love with Hillary."

"I know that."

"How could I marry someone else and think it would all be okay?" He sipped his coffee again. "Dad, Hillary is pregnant."

His father had lifted his mug to his lips but paused before sipping. "The timing seems unfortunate for you."

Chase chuckled and shook his head. "Well, the fact is, it's my baby."

His father's eyes widened and then softened. "Well that doesn't seem so strange does it. Fate maybe?"

"She doesn't want anything to do with me."

"Oh, I doubt that."

"I didn't want to have kids like this, where the parents aren't together."

His father sat back in his chair. "Well, you can hold a grudge, or you can look at the rest of your life. You turned out okay, and you and I have always been okay. I did what I could to keep you and your siblings together, on my side that is."

And he had. Chase knew this was his issue and he had to deal with it. "What do I do?"

His father leaned in and covered Chase's hands with his own. "You said it. You love her."

"I do."

"Then tell her again."

"She kicked me out." He shook his head. "Okay, she kicked me out because I think I inadvertently called her a whore and didn't mean to."

His father laughed and sat back. "I'd have kicked you out too. Chase, you're quick with the temper and slow in the patience. But this is going to need some. Give her a few days, and then sweep her off her feet. I know she loves you. Who wouldn't?"

CHAPTER 32

C hase had done as his father had said, and he waited a few days. Against his better judgement, he'd even called Tammi to check on her. She confirmed that he was still an asshole and she never wanted to see him again.

He was used to that and he could carry on knowing that was how things would be.

What he couldn't carry on with was Hillary hating him, and he'd been the biggest jackass of all to her.

A baby—with Hillary. Just thinking about it filled his heart. He'd never wanted to be a father—okay, he'd never thought about it. And even standing outside the chapel with Tammi, he'd never thought about marrying anyone either—except Hillary.

The signs were everywhere, and now he was just mad. Why hadn't he fought harder when she pushed him away?

He sipped the beer he held in one hand and looked at the ring in the box he held in his other. It was almost as beautiful as she was, he thought.

When the woman at the jewelry store asked him about Hillary, he described the auburn color of her hair and the flecks of gold in her green eyes. The golden hue of her skin, and the dimple that formed when she smiled sweetly.

The woman took those words and escorted him to a setting that he felt matched her exactly.

Chase knew it wasn't about the ring, and that wasn't what would win her over. There was more to it. He loved her, and deep down inside he knew she knew that. And, they were going to have a baby.

HILLARY WALKED toward the store on Monday morning. She juggled her bags and her purse trying to find her keys. It had taken her longer to get ready that morning because suddenly, nothing fit. Her stomach showed now, and anyone that knew her would know what was going on. It was a good thing the cat had been let out of the bag before then.

Finally finding the keys, she hiked the bags up on her shoulders, and unlocked the door. When she pushed it open, the fragrance hit her first. Then she noticed the rose petals scattered through the store, and when she followed them with her eyes, at the end of them was Chase.

He was in a suit, but not his driving suit, and he was down on one knee.

"What are you doing here?" She looked around. "Where is Kennedy?"

He smiled up at her. "This isn't for Kennedy."

Hillary walked toward him, still unsure as to why he was there. Okay, she knew, but why?

The closer she got to him she realized there was a ring in the box that he held in his hand. She bit down on her lip to keep it from trembling. "Chase?"

"I should have argued a little harder that Sunday morning when you were washing the champagne glasses in the break room. The morning I was enjoying placing little kisses on your skin, and you turned me away." He stood and walked to her. "I should have followed the I love you up with reasons, and so much more. I should have been the first person you told that you were carrying my baby because I should have been there."

Hillary pressed her hand to her heart. "You love me?"

"I told you I loved you."

"But you've always loved me—as a friend."

Chase reached his hand out and cupped her cheek. "That's what I kept telling myself, but it was just something that was comforting to me when I was sure you didn't want me."

Hillary batted tears back and her lips and hands trembled. "I've always wanted you. I just never wanted to hurt Kennedy."

"Don't use me as an excuse," they heard Kennedy's voice from the back and they both broke out in laughter.

"I can't do anything without her," he smiled and held up the ring. "Hillary, you're the one and only woman I've ever wanted and five years ago, I thought I would have a chance, but I wasn't ready. Three months ago, I didn't want to let you go. And now, there is so much more at stake, and I want you even more." He pressed his hand to her stomach, and Hillary covered it with her own. An energy she'd never felt before surged through her, as if the baby were right there with them. "Marry me, Hillary. We're a family, you and me. We should have always been together."

"Are you sure you want only me for the rest of your life?"

He pulled her closer. "It's the only thing in my life I know for certain. So, what do you say? Will you marry me?"

Hillary felt the teeniest flutter in her belly. She knew he hadn't felt it, but she had. Was that the baby, or was it the bliss she was feeling after the past few months?

"Of course I will. I love you too much to ever let you go again."

Chase pulled her closer and placed a kiss on her lips that

made her sway. Then he took the ring from the box and slipped it on her finger. "You've made me incredibly happy, Hillary."

"I'm happy too."

Chase bent and kissed her slight baby bump and she thought her heart might explode, only this time it was because she was so happy.

He kissed her again and pressed his forehead to hers. "Should I leave my sister back there a little longer?"

"No. I want to see you both," Kennedy's voice rang out from the back again and they both laughed as she and Joel, Max and Paige, and their father rushed to congratulate them.

When Hillary finally broke free of everyone's embraces, she had a moment to step back and look at the ring Chase had given her. An emerald surrounded by diamonds. It was the most beautiful thing she'd ever seen in her life.

CHAPTER 33

There was a nearly full moon outside Hillary's window, and when the wind blew through the leaves on the trees it made beautiful patterns on the ceiling. In the stillness of the night, she held her hand up in the shimmer of moonlight and admired the ring Chase had given her.

They were engaged—her and Chase. The very thought of it made her heart full.

Chase's hand came to her stomach, and like before, there was a fluttering. He rolled closer to her, pressing a kiss to her neck.

"Your bed is more comfortable than mine," he whispered.

"My room is cleaner."

"I cleaned mine," he said as he maneuvered his arm under her so he held her against him. "After our night together, I cleaned my house. And it's stuck."

"I'll have to see it to believe it."

"My bed tomorrow."

Hillary laced her fingers with his and rested them on her belly. "You being here feels surreal. I feel like I should be pinched or something."

Chase took that to heart and pinched her shoulder with the arm he held around her.

"Ow," she laughed. "Okay, this is real."

Chase adjusted again so that he was balanced over her, looking down at her with those amazing eyes. "This is how it should have always been. Hell, we should have known this clear back in high school."

"We wouldn't have appreciated what we have until now."

Chase pressed a kiss to her lips. "A baby. We're going to have a baby together. I hope that she looks just like you."

A part of her heart melted when he said that. "I was thinking a little boy who looked just like you would be amazing."

"I love you, Hillary. I can't remember a day when I didn't love you."

She lifted her hands into his hair. "I've always loved you, too. We just had to wait for our time."

Chase shimmied down her body, leaving kisses between her breasts and down to her belly where he stopped. He lingered a kiss just below her bellybutton. "I love you too, little one. I won't miss a day of your life. I promise."

Hillary felt the tears welling in her eyes, but she didn't want to cry. This was such a perfect moment; she didn't want to mar it with hormonal emotion. But her body didn't care, and the tears fell.

She wiped them away as quickly as she could, but he'd seen them.

Chase moved until he was next to her and he scooped her up in his arms. "Why the tears?"

"Because everything makes me cry. Everything."

"But this is happy. I mean Kennedy wants me here. We have her blessing. We have my dad's blessing. Hell, we have my mom's blessing, and your mom's blessing. There's no reason for tears."

"I'm so glad you won't miss any more of this. Of course, all you missed was me getting sick."

"I didn't miss that. Remember? I was there for that."

She smiled. "You were. I guess we have a lot to think about. Where are we going to live? Are we going to get married before the baby gets here? Are we going to wait? When will we even have time for a honeymoon?"

Chase laughed and pressed a kiss to the top of her head.

"Your house is nicer, but mine has enough space for the cars. Though, Max did say, if I was willing to foot the bill on it, I could put a garage on his construction lot."

"And what would you do with a garage?"

"Oh, the things I could do. All of the cars would be locked inside when not in use. I would hire a mechanic that would work on them, instead of me farming out the jobs. We could detail them there. It's a win, win."

Hillary turned to face him. "I have a nice little nest egg. Maybe we can use it to build that garage. And, since I like my house better, we could sell yours, pay off your sister, and update this house to get ready for the baby."

Chase brushed her hair back and kissed her hard on the mouth. "Listen to us making grown up plans for the future, and a baby."

"Who knew it would be possible?"

"What kind of wedding and honeymoon? You deserve the best, Hill. I mean it. The best."

Hillary rested her hand on her taut tummy. "I have the best. And now I finally have you."

"You always had me. That was my whole problem." He kissed her again. "Now, what kind of wedding?"

"You know, my Barbies had some elaborate weddings. I used to dress up like Princess Diana and I assumed I'd marry someone cuter than the prince." He chuckled at that, but her eyes warned there was more. "I always thought I'd have a tiara when I got married and a long train on my dress. And not a stitch of pink in the whole place, but that decision came when I got older."

"I can't imagine why," he teased.

"But, honestly, now, none of that is important. Chase, I'd marry you in the back yard."

"We can do better than that."

"Can we? I don't want to wait. And I'm not Princess Diana, I'm not Barbie, and I'm not your sister. Though, I have to admit, she had the most perfect wedding and she didn't fuss over it too much."

"That surprised you too?"

"Especially since I know she only found out she was pregnant an hour before her wedding." Hillary sighed at the memory of it. "Oh, I know what we should do."

"What?"

This time she pushed him onto his back and straddled him. Her hair falling over her shoulders. "Let's have a surprise party."

Chase held his hands on her hips. "What kind of surprise would it be if we knew about it?"

She laughed and shook her head. "No. We'll surprise everyone by inviting them to a location and having a wedding. Oh, God, won't that be awesome."

"Every day for the rest of my life, it's going to be an adventure, isn't it?"

"I hope so. And the best part, we'll never have to be awkward around each other again."

Chase pulled her down to him and they made love again, in the bed they would share forever.

CHAPTER 34

There was a different bounce in Hillary's step the next morning. She felt it from the tips of her toes to the top of her head.

Her gaze continually moved to her finger and the ring that adorned it. Bliss, was that what she was feeling? In all her life, she'd never been so happy.

When she unlocked the door to the store, she could hear the music already playing, the kind that soothed customers into browsing. New jewelry had been set out, which meant that Kennedy had been creating. Voices carried from the break room, and when Hillary walked through the doorway, she let out a little gasp, and then a giggle when she saw Kennedy and Joel in a heated kiss, just as she had nearly a year earlier.

The moment the noise escaped her throat she wanted to retreat, leave them to their privacy, but they pulled apart and Kennedy's cheeks went pink.

"I'm sorry. I didn't mean to interrupt," she apologized, still wanting to back out of the room.

Joel pulled his wife to him and held her there. "Can't get enough of her," he said lovingly. "Isn't she beautiful?"

His hands had come to her stomach, which Hillary realized had grown in size over the weekend.

"You do have a glow to you, Ken."

Kennedy waved off the comment and kissed her husband quickly on the lips. "Go to work now. We have shipments coming."

Joel bent down and kissed Kennedy's stomach and then her lips. "I'll see you ladies later."

They watched as he let himself out the back door.

Kennedy turned, and her eyes steadied on Hillary. "You're still engaged? Nothing happed overnight that changed anything, right?"

Hillary held up her hand to show her that the ring was still in place. "I don't know if I should take offense to that question or not."

"Honestly, I can't say it was aimed at you. It might have been aimed at my brother."

Her brother—the thought of him made Hillary's heart race. "We had the most amazing night. And the best part is, I don't have to keep it a secret."

Kennedy picked up her tea mug from the table and moved toward Hillary. "You never should have had to. Imagine the years of bliss you could have had without me in your way."

She passed by Hillary and walked to her office. Setting the mug on the table, she kicked off her shoes, and sat down at her desk.

Hillary followed her, stopping in the doorway, leaning against the doorjamb. "We weren't ready. Now we are. I've never been so happy in all my life."

Kennedy looked up at her and studied her face. "I believe you." She eased back in her chair, resting her hands on her stomach. "What kind of plans did you make for your future in the arms of the man you love?"

Kennedy's poetic statement had Hillary laughing. "You assume we made plans?"

"I assume you didn't get but a few hours of sleep last night. You have dark circles under your eyes, even though they are sparkling out of pure joy. But I know what it is to resolve that you're in love and everything is perfect. And you've waited years for this moment."

A smile tugged at Hillary's cheeks. "We did make plans. Or discussed them. Living arrangements for us and his cars," she giggled. "Wedding plans, baby plans, remod..."

"Wedding plans?" Kennedy interrupted. "That's what I want to hear about."

"I don't have anything to share—yet. But you'll be the first to know." Hillary eased from the doorjamb. "By the way, we're having a barbecue at our house on Sunday at three. Bring a side dish?"

Kennedy nodded slowly. "*Our house*," she mimicked.

"Yes, which is my house. You'll be there?"

"Of course."

"Good. FedEx just pulled up. I'll go get the boxes and start inventorying."

CHASE KNOCKED on his father's door, again with bagels in his hand and a tray with two coffees. He was more than surprised when Gloria answered.

"Chase, what a nice surprise," she said as she opened the door for him to step inside.

"I think I should be saying that. I didn't know you were coming back."

"I thought it would be nicer if I drove out with your father instead of him driving down alone. Besides, the movers come

Monday, and he's not done packing," she whispered and then smiled. "What did you bring?"

Chase looked at the bag in his hand and the tray in the other. "I brought bagels and coffee. I would have brought more if..."

"Hush, we will make do. I'm very happy to see you, and I hear congratulations are in order," she said as they walked toward the kitchen. "You and Hillary?"

"Yes. I guess they are."

"A wedding and a baby," she sighed. "It's all wonderful news. Your father told me about you two, and even when we met, he mentioned that he thought she'd be good for you. But, well, that was before any of this came up."

Chase smiled at the thought that he and Hillary were meant to be, and everyone knew it. It just took them a while to figure it out themselves.

As surprised as Chase was to see Gloria open the door, he was more surprised to see his father in the kitchen, on a step stool, pulling down items from a top shelf and setting them in a moving box.

"Chase," he said as he climbed down. "I'm going to take this as a sign you're going to miss me. I've seen you more in the past few weeks than I have in thirty-six years."

He knew his father saw the humor in that, but it twisted a knife into Chase's chest. He should have been showing up with bagels and coffees the whole time.

"Yeah, it'll be weird with you gone."

His father shrugged, grabbed the kitchen towel off the counter, and wiped off his hands. "You'll be busy. A bride and a baby. I'm really proud of you, son."

Chase wasn't a man that cried, but right then, he thought he could have bawled like a baby.

Gloria moved past his father, and Chase watched as he followed her with his eyes. His father was in love, and that eased that earlier pain that his father had put into Chase's chest.

"You boys sit down. I'll divide this all up," Gloria said as she pulled a cutting board out of a box and began cutting up the bagels.

Chase's father pulled out a chair and motioned for him to sit in the other. "What brings you by?"

Chase sat down across from his father. "I came to invite you to a barbecue on Sunday, at three at Hillary's house—our house."

"A barbecue? That sounds like a good time."

"I think so. And, Gloria, of course you're invited as well."

She turned with the plate of bagels cut up into bite sizes and carried them to the table. "I appreciate that. What can I bring?"

Chase shrugged. "Hillary said a side dish, but I don't know what that entails, really."

Gloria rested her hand on his arm. "I'll figure out something. What's the occasion?"

He did everything he could to keep the smile from surfacing on his lips, including shoving a piece of bagel into his mouth. "Now that we're a little family, we thought it would be nice to have family over."

Gloria pressed her hand to her chest. "That's precious. We'll be there."

CHAPTER 35

I t had been a long time since Hillary had had a party at her house. They'd bought some patio furniture and a few extra chairs. Chase had surprised her with a small pergola for them to decorate and get married under.

She'd bought a nice, white, springtime dress for the ceremony, and was creative enough to make a head wreath out of daisies in lieu of a veil.

Chase was still messing with the new grill when she walked out onto the patio in her dress, her hair piled atop her head in curls, adorned with the daisy wreath.

He stopped what he was doing and stared at her. "You are the most beautiful woman in the world. I can't believe you're all mine," he said moving toward her and stopping short of touching her. "I don't want to mess up your dress."

"Do you have it all working?" she asked looking past him to the grill.

"It's all ready. Joel offered to do the cooking, and I took him up on it. I'd rather be right next to you all day."

"I can't believe I'll be your wife soon."

He moved in and pressed a kiss to her lips without touching

his hands to her. "You should have been my wife years ago," he said before he went into the house to clean up.

Hillary rested her hands on the small bump of a belly. "He loves us," she said to the baby. "Everything is so perfect right now."

An hour later, Hillary and Chase stood at the side gate to their back yard waiting to greet their guests. Kennedy, Joel, and Paige had all arrived at the same time. Kennedy carried a large bowl, no doubt of potato salad, and Paige had a box, which Hillary assumed was a cake of some kind.

"Don't you look beautiful," Kennedy said as she walked toward them. Then she shifted her eyes to her brother. "And you look handsome."

Chase took the bowl from her. "Thank you. Hillary has something for you."

Hillary turned to the small table they had set up by the gate filled with daisies. "You each get a flower," she said as she took one and pinned it to Joel's polo shirt, and then one on the straps of both Kennedy and Paige's dresses.

Paige pulled her glasses down her nose and studied Hillary over the top of them. "Why are we wearing flowers?"

"Because it's a very special day."

Hillary and Chase repeated the greeting with each of their guests. And each guest eyed them curiously.

Gloria had brought a dessert salad, and Hillary hugged her when she cried after receiving her flower. "I'm sorry. I get emotional when people do sweet things like this. If I didn't know better, I'd think I was at a wedding."

Chase and Hillary exchanged looks and laughed but didn't say anything more. Hillary escorted Gloria to the kitchen with her salad, and Chase's father moved in to speak to him.

"I saw your mother parking her car up the street. I didn't know she was going to be here," he said.

Chase was ready for this. "Is that a problem?"

"I just didn't get to warn Gloria."

"Mom isn't going to cause a scene or anything. You've always done well when she was married to someone else. Kennedy's mom and her husband are here."

"Yeah, I'm used to them being together. I guess I've never been the one with a plus one," he chuckled. "Should I talk to her first? Tell her about Gloria?"

Chase kissed his father on the cheek. "I'll tell her. Everything is going to be okay."

His father nodded and narrowed his gaze on him. "This isn't just a barbecue, is it?"

Chase rested a hand on his father's shoulder and smiled. "I'm happy, Dad. No matter what happens today, know that I'm the happiest I've ever been in my entire life."

"Hillary does that to you."

"She most certainly does."

His father continued into the yard, and Chase waited for his mother.

"You're greeting us at the side of the house? Whose house is this anyway? This isn't your house. Did you move and not tell me?"

Chase smiled. She wasn't going to ruin his day. "This is Hillary's house, Mom." He kissed her on the cheek and took the bag of potato chips from her hand. "I see that your brother and sisters are here. Did you invite your other siblings too?"

He bit down on his cheek to keep from saying something unkind. "No. Hillary is Kennedy's best friend. She doesn't know my other siblings."

"If you're going to marry the woman, don't you think you should introduce them?"

"In time, Mom. And I guess I should tell you, but no one else knows yet. We're going to get married today. Here, in the yard."

Her eyes went wide. "Now? You're getting married now? You should have told me. I'm in shorts, Chase Michael. This is embarrassing."

"It shouldn't be. Kennedy's husband is in shorts and so is Max."

"I'm sure they don't look like they just showed up for a game of horseshoes."

"We didn't tell anyone what we were doing. This is our surprise. Hillary and I didn't want to wait to get married. We wanted to have everything in order before the baby came."

When his mother's eyes grew even wider, he realized they didn't really talk at all. "Baby?"

"Yes. We're having a baby in November."

She pressed her hand to her chest. "I suppose your father knew all about this?"

"He's been around for it, yes. He knows Hillary, and he's very happy for us."

"I don't know why you can't include me in your life, Chase. I just don't think this is something you've thought out."

"I have. It's what I want."

"A baby out of marriage is not easy."

"We'll be married. And, Mom, Hillary and I have been with each other since junior high school,. I mean as friends. This isn't someone I just met and took home."

She must have felt attacked, he decided when the tears began to roll down her cheeks. "I think I'm going to go home. You don't need me here."

"I invited you here."

"And kept it all a secret."

"It's a surprise for everyone, Mom. Even Hillary's mom doesn't know what we're doing. Well, I think they're all starting to suspect, but you're the only one that knows."

She worried her bottom lip. "Your father is here?"

"Yes. He and his girlfriend just arrived."

"Girlfriend?" she choked out the word. "I've never known him to have a girlfriend."

"I think this is the first one since Leah died."

He knew that hit hard, because his father had loved Leah more than he'd ever loved anyone, and his mother knew that. "So, I'm just some unhappy woman walking into a blissful party. Is his ex-wife still married to that man?"

Oh, she was petty, Chase thought. "Yes. So why don't you come in, meet everyone, and stay and watch me marry the woman I love?"

"Because I don't think you know how to love, Chase. I think you're making a big mistake."

There were a million things he wanted to say to his mother in that moment. But he knew that words she was spewing at him weren't for him. She'd never been happy in her marriages and her affairs hadn't gone well either. He hadn't invited his other siblings because he didn't know them like he knew Kennedy, Paige, and Max. Her life, and her shortcomings, weren't Chase's fault. It had taken him a lot of years to realize that, but now he did. She wouldn't make him second guess the love he had for Hillary or their baby.

"Mom, I love you. I'm glad you came, but I know you'll be uncomfortable. So, why don't you go back home. Hillary and I will have you over when there aren't a lot of people here. I want you to get to know her. And, I know you'll want to get to know your grandbaby too."

Her eyes went wide, and then narrowed. "You're dismissing me."

"I'm offering you an out."

She hiked her purse up on her shoulder. "Fine. I'll talk to you later."

Without another word, she turned and headed back to her car as Hillary walked toward him.

"Where is she going?"

Chase wrapped his arm around her waist and held the bag of chips his mother had brought in his other hand. "She doesn't think I know how to love and she's a bit put off by us getting married this way."

Hillary rested her head on his shoulder. "Chase, I'm sorry."

"Don't be. Gloria is ecstatic to be here, and she doesn't even know why." He kissed the top of her head. "The people who are most important in my life are here. And in a few minutes, you're going to take my last name. In a few months, we'll be parents. In a few years, we'll have even more kids." He turned to her and wrapped her in his arms. "I do know how to love. I've loved you since I was thirteen."

"Chase..."

"I have. No woman ever compared to you, and that was the problem. Now it's not a problem anymore. I'm never going to be bitter like that, or angry either. I promise you the best life I can give you, Hill."

"C'mon," she said easing back from his embrace and taking his hand. "Let's go make this final. I'm tired of not being your wife."

CHAPTER 36

Their families had begun to mingle while Chase had been dealing with his mother. Joel had brought beers, and Kennedy, who didn't know how not to please people, was serving glasses of wine and water.

Chase looked around the small yard and thought that this was the happiest he'd been in all his life. These were the people that had made him. These were the people who had always loved him and taught him how to love.

He wrapped his arm around Hillary's waist. "Everyone. Can we have your attention?"

The chatter stopped and all eyes turned toward him. It was time to announce their big surprise.

"Hillary and I would like to thank you for coming to celebrate with us."

"Celebrate?" Max asked. "I thought we were eating."

Chase chuckled. "You are going to eat, but we have more planned. Hillary and I have never done things in the normal way. We took the longest route possible to finally get to this place we're in, with a baby, and then our engagement, and today we've invited you here to be part of our wedding."

He noticed Gloria wipe her eyes as his father wrapped his arm around her shoulders.

"So, since everything else about Hillary and I has been a surprise, we thought a surprise wedding was in order as well."

Kennedy pressed her fingers to her lips. "Now? This is your wedding?"

Hillary nodded. "I don't want big. I don't want fancy. I just want to be surrounded by the people I love when I marry your brother."

Kennedy moved to her and enveloped her in a hug, and then pulled Chase into the fold. "I'm so happy for you both. Oh, God! A wedding. What can I do? Where can I help?"

Chase laughed and kissed his sister on the cheek. "You can pull up a chair next to your husband. Let's get this wedding started."

Everyone pulled a chair to the lawn and under Kennedy's supervision, they arranged them in front of the pergola. Chase's employee Dale stood under the pergola with them, as their officiant, as he'd been ordained on the internet.

Dale began the ceremony, but Chase wasn't sure he heard anything he said. It was all filler until the moment they were husband and wife, and they signed that paper.

"Hillary, do you have vows that you would like to say?"

Hillary took a deep breath. "Where do I begin? In the seventh grade, when I met Kennedy, and she told me you were her brother, I knew then you were going to be very important in my life. I also had a little crush on you, but I never told your sister that." They both looked at Kennedy who cried as she clung to the arm of her husband. "We knew each other through all the awkward years, and still, when you'd look at me, I'd get butterflies. Nothing changed the older I got. And now, here we are, the start of forever. I love you, Chase Devereaux."

Chase lifted his hand to caress Hillary's cheek. "You had a crush on me?"

He watched as her cheeks pinked. "Yes."

"Damn, we wasted a lot of time," he said gazing into her eyes.

"Chase," Dale said pulling his attention away from his bride. "Do you have vows you want to share?"

Chase, his hand still on Hillary's cheek, placed his other hand on her stomach. "Everything in the world is changing, and I couldn't be happier for it," he said as he then took her hands in his. "My sister's best friend had a crush on me. That has to be the coolest thing I ever heard, because, like I told you before, I've loved you as long as I can remember. I can love. And I can show love. I will forever be true to you. I promise to take care of you and our family, Hill. There is nothing now that will ever pull me away from you."

"Way to go, dude," Dale said nodding his head. "Okay. Do you have rings?"

Chase laughed as he pulled a band from his pocket and slid it on Hillary's finger next to the emerald he had given her earlier in the week. She pulled a gold band off her thumb and slid it on his finger.

"Damn, Devereaux. That's the sexiest thing you've ever owned," she whispered.

"And I'm never taking it off."

Dale chuckled. "Now, do you, Chase, take Hillary as your wife?"

"Oh, hell yeah I do," he said, and he heard his family laugh.

"Hillary, are you sure you take Chase..."

"Yes. Yes. Yes!" she said before pulling him to her and planting a long kiss on him.

Chase wrapped his arms around her and pulled her in close, deepening the kiss as Dale cleared his throat, but they didn't stop.

"Well, folks, here are Mr. and Mrs. Chase Devereaux."

There was no walking down the aisle or receiving guests in a line. Everyone who was seated in their yard stood and moved to them, hugging and kissing them.

The rest of the afternoon was filled with family and food. Joel manned the grill and Paige and Kennedy planned a baby shower for Hillary.

That night as they lay wrapped in each other's arms, Hillary sighed. "I have never been so happy in my whole. life. And last week I was throwing the biggest pity party for myself."

Chase chose not to think of the week before. How could he have thought that marrying someone other than Hillary would have ever been a good thing? No, he was as blissful as she was.

"What do you think the baby is? Boy or girl?"

Hillary took his hand and rested it on her belly. "I can't decide. Sometimes I get a girl vibe, but then I think of how sweet a little boy like you would be."

"You knew me. I wasn't a sweet little boy."

"But ours would be. Ours will be a mama's boy, but in a good way. You know, like he loves his mama more than anyone in the world."

The thought twisted in his gut. He had never been a mama's boy. Hell, he'd never even been friendly with his mom. What kind of effect would that have on his own child?

Maybe he'd go to her tomorrow and make amends. One thing was for sure, he wanted to start this new leg of his life with no regrets.

CHAPTER 37

As soon as Hillary and Kennedy had closed shop, they walked over to the tap house.

Hillary looked down at her wedding ring and Kennedy laughed. "It's been two weeks, and you're still looking at your ring?"

"I'm still surprised it's on my finger."

Kennedy laughed. "Why are you surprised? You're fifteen weeks pregnant."

"Yeah, well that doesn't surprise me as much as being married to Chase. Seriously, it's still surreal."

"You know what I think is surreal? I changed my last name and now you have it." Kennedy laughed again. "We're legally sisters and we're having babies just weeks apart."

"I love him, Ken. It feels good to be able to say that to you."

"I'm sorry you felt like you never could. Sincerely, it was never my business."

They walked through the back door and to the table that Joel had reserved for them. There were two food trucks for the night. Kennedy thought the pizza truck sounded best, but Hillary opted for fried cheese sticks from the burger truck.

When their orders came up, they carried the food back to the table, and Joel and Chase sat down with them.

"We have something for you," Kennedy said as Hillary bit down on a long string of hot cheese and pulled it until it broke free.

"For me?"

"For both of you. Before the baby gets here, you need to take a vacation. So, here." Kennedy handed Hillary an envelope.

Chase draped his arm over her shoulders as she opened it. "No kidding?" he said as he looked at brochure Hillary had pulled from the envelope.

"We can't take this. It's too much," Hillary protested as Chase took the brochure from her hands.

"We can too," he argued as he looked at the brochure of the vacation cottage in San Francisco. "Look at this, a bakery down the street. Trolley cars. We could visit Alcatraz."

Kennedy placed her hand over Hillary's. "If it makes you feel better, the cottage is owned by one of my favorite designers. She gave me a fantastic deal on it. The air mileage is from the tap house. They use one of those airline cards to buy their inventory and have lots of points."

Hillary laughed. "That does make me feel better."

"And it's in two weeks. It doesn't give you a lot of time to plan, but we had to get the cottage when it was available. I hope you can manage the time, Chase."

"I can do it."

Hillary shook her head. "But you'll be alone in the store."

"I've been alone in the store many times. And when you get back then we can finalize your baby shower, and you can finalize mine."

～

CHASE ARRANGED for Dale to pick them up in the newest of the limos, the one that Hillary had crawled through when he'd bought it.

As she relaxed in it, her husband's arm draped over her shoulders in the early morning light, she suddenly had the worst feelings wash over her. How many women had he been with in the back of the cars that he drove every day? In one month they had decided that the two times they had been together was worth a lifetime of commitment. That and the surprise that grew in her belly. But were they really different now? Could two people change that quickly?

Did he think of all the women he'd driven in that limo? Did he miss it? What about Tammi? Hell, he was going to go off and marry her.

She squeezed her eyes shut. But he hadn't married Tammi. He'd left her at the altar and raced home to Hillary—even before he knew the baby was his.

Why was she even thinking about all of this? The ring on her finger said he was promised to her forever, and hadn't he said that?

"Hey, what's wrong?" Chase's finger came under her chin and she shifted her watery gaze to him. "Why are you crying?"

"Nothing." She wiped at her cheeks. "It's nothing."

Chase turned her toward him. "You're crying. That's not nothing." He rolled the privacy window up between them and Dale. "Is everything okay? You're okay? The baby's okay?"

Hillary wiped her eyes again. "Do you love me?"

"What kind of joke is that?"

"I mean it. Do you love me?"

"Yes, I love you and I think I made that quite clear. We're married. We're having a baby."

"But you were going to marry Tammi."

He eased back, and she'd seen the flicker of mad in his eyes. "I was going to marry Tammi, because I thought I couldn't have you, damnit. Are you really bringing this up as we are heading off to our honeymoon?"

"And did you have sex with Tammi in this car?"

Now the flicker in his eyes deepened and his cheeks turned red. Was this what she wanted? Was she stirring for a fight?

"What is this about? Why in the hell are you bringing this up? We've been married for a month. You're questioning me on this now?"

"I want to know."

"I don't want to discuss it," he argued and sat back, crossing his arms in front of him.

"You did," she cried. "You had sex with her in this car. Right here?"

His lip trembled as he tried to control his anger. "Hillary, don't do this."

"Did you even love her?"

"I have never loved anyone but you." His voice cracked as it rose. "I don't know what kind of game you're playing here, but I don't like it. We both have a past, Hill. We were always open about that. Yes, you know I had my share of women and don't go playing all sweet and innocent on me. I know you had your share of men. Already, this marriage is the longest relationship either of us has had. So knock it off."

"You didn't answer my question. Did you love her, and did you have sex with her here?"

Chase ran his hand over his mouth. "Yes. We had sex in this car. And no, I never did love her. Are you happy now? Is that what you absolutely had to know?"

The tears came harder now, and Hillary wrapped her arms around her stomach, causing Chase to move in.

"Hillary, talk to me. Are you okay?"

"No. I can't stop crying. I can't stop worrying about it. I know you had sex with her in the car. I know it wasn't special. I know you love me and always have. Maybe this is hormonal. I don't know. There's a deep-seated need to be mad at you over everything, and all the while I know it's stupid because I love you and you love me."

"Well, as stupid as it all is, at least you're rational."

She pressed her head to his chest and chuckled. "Why does this come over me?"

"Because you're growing a person in you and you're having to share everything with them. I'm not going to let you push me away again, Hill. You can't do it. Not this time."

"Keep telling me that. I have a feeling I'm going to keep trying. Hormones suck."

Chase chuckled and kissed the top of her head. "I'll fight for you forever."

CHAPTER 38

The Monday morning after Hillary returned from her honeymoon, she walked through the front door of Kennedy's store in her cotton summer dress that Chase had bought her on the pier.

She'd picked at least three more fights with him while they were gone, but he'd managed to defuse them all. She owed him the credit he was due for that.

As usual, Kennedy was in her office, seated behind her desk. Her bare feet making circles in the plush pink carpet under her chair.

"Good morning," she said to draw Kennedy's attention to her.

Kennedy turned in her chair, and Hillary could have sworn she was twice the size she'd been when they'd left on their honeymoon.

"The newlywed is back. How was San Fran?"

Hillary leaned against the doorjamb and rested her hand on her belly. "It was beautiful, Ken. I will never be able to thank you guys enough for what you did for us."

"You're happy. That's thanks enough."

Hillary nodded, but when Kennedy's head tilted, she knew her face didn't register her happiness.

"You're not happy. What's wrong?" Kennedy asked as she stood from behind her desk.

"I just don't feel like myself. Is it hormonal?"

Kennedy laughed and passed by her, placing her hand on Hillary's arm, encouraging her to follow her to the break room.

Hillary followed and watched as Kennedy took two mugs from the cupboard and filled them from the tap that Joel had installed on the sink for instant hot water. She carried the mugs to the table and sat down next to the basket of teas they had now, in lieu of the pots of coffee they would normally drink.

"Sit down and join me," she instructed Hillary, who complied. "Your body is growing another human. Not only a human, but it's part you and part Chase." She laughed. "Imagine the internal fight going on there."

Hillary held in her giggle and pulled a mug toward her. "Are you saying my baby is a demon?"

"I'm saying your body is adjusting. What's going on?"

Hillary chose a tea bag, decaffeinated, as they all were, she noticed. She opened it and dunked it into the water. "I keep picking fights with him."

"Normal."

"On the way to the airport, I ripped into him about having sex with Tammi in the back of the limo."

Kennedy halted her bobbing of her tea bag to study her. "That couldn't have gone over well."

"He handled it well, I thought. I pushed him until he finally said they had had sex there. But I knew that. And that was a different time. He's loyal to me, and hell, hasn't he said he's always sort of been?"

"He's always loved you. Any time spent apart was my fault," Kennedy admitted.

"I don't think it was. I think we both needed to mature to be together. We were brought up different. I wasn't done having fun either. Not that Chase isn't fun," she began to back pedal and Kennedy covered her hand with hers.

"I understand what you mean."

"But I picked more fights on the honeymoon, and even one this morning."

"And how does Chase handle that?"

Hillary laughed now, taking a spoon and assaulting the tea bag with it. "Oh, he's calm He listens to me spew hateful things at him and accuse him of things he's not doing, then he says something calm and pulls me in and tells me I'm okay. But I'm not okay, Ken. Something is wrong with me."

"Let me repeat, you're growing a human."

"I love him. I love him so much it hurts sometimes."

"What a glorious feeling, huh?"

"So why am I doing this?"

"I wonder the same thing," Chase's voice came from behind them and they both turned to see him in the doorway. "Your bell doesn't seem to do any good. There is a woman looking at a purse out here. You might want to help her."

Kennedy's eyes went wide and she hurried out of the room as Chase took her seat.

"What are you doing here?" Hillary asked as she pushed the ceremonial tea to the center of the table.

"I came to check on you. I have a ride to the airport in an hour, so I thought I'd stop by."

"How is it you don't run from me? I'm so horrible to you."

He brushed her hair back from her face. "No you're not. You're having our baby and it'll do this to you. I've been reading up on it."

Again, she knew her expression gave away her thoughts when he laughed.

Chase eased back in his seat and pulled her tea toward him. "I read," he said as he lifted the mug to his lips, sniffed, and then set it back down without tasting it. "I want to help you through this. Do you think I'm only going to want one baby?"

Now the tears started. It was a vicious cycle. "I don't know if I can handle that."

"You can. You're absolutely amazing. And you'll forget all about this."

"But will you? Why do I keep accusing you and confronting you?"

"I was thinking about that, and Hill, my track record speaks for itself. Honestly, sometimes when you call me out, I wonder why you agreed to marry me."

"Because I love you."

"Yeah, and then I remember that." He eased in toward her and took her hands in his. "And I love you, so I'll forever be honest and faithful to you. And, every time you attack me, I'll defuse it and hold you. We're in this together for the long haul, and not because we have to be—because we want to be."

"You're right. I don't want to be anywhere but with you."

"Good." He leaned in and pressed a kiss to her lips as Kennedy cleared her throat behind them.

"That was a funny thing you did there. You could have warned me that you brought your mom into the store," she scowled.

"Didn't buy the purse?"

"Too expensive. So she touched a few more things and then said she was going home."

"I figured she came to share her joyous attitude." He shifted his eyes back to Hillary. "I think she's trying to find a way to talk to you, but she doesn't know how."

Hillary sat back and rested her hands on her stomach, which tensed at the very thought. "She wants to talk to me?"

"Well, she and I haven't been able to have much of a conversation on our own without arguing."

"I don't know..."

"You don't have to either. I can tell her to stay clear of you until you're ready."

Hillary drew in a deep breath. "No. I'll go to her. I have no ill will toward her and I want her to know her grandchild."

"I think that's what she wants, she just doesn't know how to go about being part of our lives."

She looked at Kennedy who smiled at her, and then to Chase, whose eyes were soft and kind.

"What kind of pastries does she like? I'll take her something sweet, and maybe things will go well."

CHAPTER 39

Hillary slowed the car as she drove down the street Chase's mom lived on. Her stomach was giving her fits, and she didn't know if it was nerves or more morning sickness—which wasn't only in the morning, she'd found out.

As she pulled toward the curb outside Judy Lowell's house, she saw her on her knees in front of her budding flower garden. Hillary drew in a long breath and let it out as she climbed from her car with the box of chocolate chip cookies, which was all the bakery had left for the day.

Judy turned her head to see who had gotten out of the car, and then she slowly rose to her feet.

"Hello, Mrs. Lowell," Hillary called out as she watched the woman scan a look over her morphed body.

"Hillary. What a surprise."

"I didn't get to see you at the boutique this morning, so I thought I might drop by and say hello. I brought chocolate chip cookies," she offered as she held out the box.

Judy bit down on her bottom lip as she reached for them.

Hillary could see that she now was out of sorts too, so they were on even ground.

"This is a nice surprise. I look a fright," she said fixing the few strands of hair that had fallen from her ponytail. "Would you like to come in for coffee? Oh, you probably don't drink coffee. Well because of the baby. Maybe some tea? I might have some herbal tea. Or juice."

"I'd love a glass of water."

"Water. I can do that."

Hillary followed Judy into her house. She hadn't been there since senior year in high school when they all posed for photos outside by the tree. The house hadn't changed much.

As they passed through the hall to the kitchen, Hillary admired the wall of photos of Judy's children. Some were married, there were grandkids, and the only photo she had of Chase was his senior picture. He truly had been an only child in a family full of children.

Judy set the box of cookies on the table and Hillary took a seat. "I was just thinking, I haven't been here since we were seniors."

"That's been a while."

"Seems like forever ago."

Judy set two glasses of water on the table and sat down. "I'm nervous having you here. I thought I should just be upfront with that."

Hillary smiled. "I'm nervous being here. I suppose we're even."

"Congratulations on the marriage and your baby. That's a big step for Chase."

"It's big for both of us. But, honestly, I can't imagine going through this with anyone else. It took us a while to figure out that we were meant to be together, but we got there."

Judy eased back in her chair. "I could have told you that years ago. You and Chase were always good together. You could ground him like no one could."

The sentiment nearly made Hillary cry. "I guess we both had to mature a little bit."

"How far along are you?"

Hillary ran her hands over her belly. "Almost eighteen weeks."

"Almost halfway there."

"I can't believe it."

Judy opened the box of cookies and set one on a napkin for each of them. "I remember when I was pregnant with Chase. I was two months pregnant before I knew, and he came three weeks early."

Hillary saw the flash of what she would consider regret in Judy's eyes. There was no regret in having Chase, but Hillary knew that his existence ripped apart two families.

"Kennedy is a few weeks ahead of me, and I don't know if watching what she goes through at each stage helps my anxiety or adds to it."

"Do you know what you're having?"

"I don't. We haven't discussed finding out. I have another ultrasound in a few weeks."

"That's exciting."

Hillary opened her purse and pulled out the copy of the first ultrasound and handed it to Judy. "I had a copy made for you. I thought you'd like to see your grandbaby."

Judy's eyes filled with tears as she looked down at the picture. "It's amazing what they can do now, isn't it?" She ran her fingers over the picture. "You don't miss a moment."

"It's rather nice." Hillary took a bite of the cookie in front of her and then set it back down. "I'm sorry we didn't tell you that the barbecue was our wedding. We just didn't want to wait."

Judy set the photo on the table and pushed it back with the tips of her fingers. "I was wrong to act like I did. Sometimes, I just get in a mood around Chase, which isn't his fault. Knowing his father and his ex-wife were there, I didn't know how to react. So, I reacted badly."

"Chase understands, and so do I. I just want you to know, you're welcome to come around any time. We want you to be a part of this."

Judy reached her hand across to cover Hillary's. "Thirty-six years later, and I'm still embarrassed by having a baby out of wedlock—well, with another man while I was still married." She let out a hard breath. "Wow, I don't think I've ever said that aloud. I'm not embarrassed by Chase, though. Out of all my kids, he's probably the most ambitious, but he was also the wildest. I've worried about him, and when all of this happened, I let that get to me—my own shortcomings."

"Chase holds no grudges toward you."

"I don't know about that," Judy laughed and eased back. "But, I think he's trying hard to be the bigger person. I appreciate you coming here and seeing me. And thank you for the picture."

"When we get a new one, I'll bring it. I also have a nice wedding portrait that Paige took."

"I should update my wall."

And that was what Hillary thought too. "I'll drop it by. I should be headed home. Thanks for letting me stay and chat."

Judy reached for Hillary's hand again. "Any time. And thank you for being there for Chase. He has always had an eye for you. I'm glad you both decided to give it a try."

CHAPTER 40

C hase was sitting on the front step when Hillary pulled up to the house. She thought he looked like a little boy who needed to talk. No doubt, he was worried about how her conversation with his mother went.

As soon as she turned off the engine, he stood and started toward her.

"You don't look as if she dragged you out back and whipped you."

Hillary laughed. "In fact, we had a delightful conversation," she said as she closed the door and walked toward him. "She just doesn't know how to react, I think. She's still embarrassed by her ways thirty-six years ago, and there was no way she could face your dad or Kennedy and Max's mom."

"Some mistakes live forever, huh?"

Hillary reached her hand to his cheek and guided his eyes to meet hers. "She doesn't think of you as a mistake. I think she's only sad that it cost two families pain, but she loves you, Chase. Don't ever think otherwise."

"Thank you for going."

"I'm glad I did. Though, I thought I was going to throw up on her lawn I was so nervous. I gave her a picture of the baby."

"Wonder where that'll end up."

Hillary wrapped her arms around her husband. "I'm sure it will hang next to our wedding photo on her wall. I'm going to get one printed for her and take it over. Maybe I'll frame it and take a nail. Would you like it to replace your senior photo, or just hang next to it?"

Chase pulled her in tighter. She knew he was grateful that she understood him. And regardless of their upbringing, they had each other now, and that was truly all that mattered.

CHASE WAS no expert in the kitchen, but he'd made dinner and it was on the table when they'd walked through the door. The smile on Hillary's face was all he was looking for. How could she not still have doubts that he'd be suitable? Even he was worried that he wasn't suitable.

"Let me change my clothes and then I'll be right out."

"Take your time," he said as he took the foil off the lasagna he'd bought at the store and warmed in the oven. The garlic bread was still in the oven to keep it warm, and the salad was waiting in the refrigerator.

When Hillary emerged from the bedroom, she had on a pair of shorts, that were unbuttoned and pushed down under her stomach, and the T-shirt she wore barely covered the front of the shorts.

"No comments," she said as she sat down at the table. "Nothing fits."

"Maybe we should buy you some things that do."

She let out a breath. "I don't know where to begin. Kennedy is wearing designer maternity clothes that the designers themselves are sending her. If I show up in a Target dress, it won't be the same."

He wanted to laugh, but he refrained and set down the salad bowl. Chase retrieved the bread from the oven and set it on the table before sitting down beside her. "We can buy you nice things, Hill. Where do you want to go?"

"I'd be comfortable in your T-shirts and a pair of elastic shorts."

He laughed. "And my sister would kick you out of her store."

"I already feel like a house. I can't imagine what I'll feel like when I'm really pregnant."

"You are really pregnant. You're halfway there. And look at Kennedy, in the next few weeks you're going—"

"To balloon up. I know." She tore a piece of bread from the loaf. "Okay, this weekend we can buy me a few things. I need to be comfortable."

"And don't even think that outfit you have on isn't perfect. The more you change the more beautiful you become."

"Do you really think so?"

"I do." He kissed her before picking up the spatula and serving her a slice of the lasagna.

THE NEXT FEW weeks were filled with them moving the rest of Chase's things from his house to their house. Hillary shopped for maternity clothes that were suitable for working at Kennedy's store, but knowing she'd be not pregnant more than she would be, she only bought a few items.

They'd scoped out Max's construction lot where he'd said Chase could build a garage for his cars, and they laid down plans to make it a reality.

When the framing was done the following month, they walked the site again.

"It'll hold four cars," Chase said as they walked hand in hand through the open building. A mechanic bay will be on the end, and we can park them doubled up."

Hillary looked at the space they stood in. "You can't park the Hummer in here and three more cars."

Chase turned her toward him. "I sold the hummer and the Cadillac. I bought two more town cars."

"But that's not what your business is."

Chase pulled her to him. "It is now. I don't need cars that seat twenty drunks in them. What I need are four cars that take people to the airport and around town, just like I do every day. I need a car anyone can drive, and I paid back my sister."

"Did you do that because..."

"Because it's the right thing to do, Hill. I was in finance for a lot of years before they let me go. I know what makes sense. I also know that as long as those big cars were in my fleet you'd worry and wonder. I'm making sure there is no reason for you to ever wonder—not that you have to."

Hillary wrapped her arms around his neck and rested her head to his chest. "I trust you, Chase."

"I know you do. It's a sound business decision for the three of us."

She giggled and lowered her hands to her belly. The baby thinks it's a good idea too.

Hillary took Chase's hand and placed it where the baby had kicked her. He hadn't had much luck feeling the movements yet, but this time, there was no mistaking the fact that he'd felt it.

"Wow."

Hillary's eyes filled with joyful tears. "I know, right?"

"It's got to be a boy. That was quite a kick."

Hillary narrowed her eyes. "Remember my soccer days? I had quite a kick."

"True. I was on the receiving end of a few of those."

"I love our history."

Chase pulled her to him again. "I love our future."

CHAPTER 41

Kennedy's baby shower was held on a Sunday in the store. Hillary and Paige had planned it, and they couldn't think of a better place to have a baby shower for a little girl other than her mother's pink palace, as they'd told Kennedy when she'd announced that they were having a girl.

Every gift that Kennedy opened made her tear up.

June Kingsley, her mother-in-law, had given her an afghan that Joel's great-grandmother had made for Joel. That seemed to be the gift that had her tears spilling over. Especially since her own mother had given her a box of diapers and a gift card to Target to buy what she wanted.

When the guests had dispersed, Kennedy sat in a chair, her feet propped up on another. Hillary watched her as she rubbed her hands over her enlarged belly.

"I just texted Joel and told him to bring the truck. You have too much stuff to put into your car," Hillary said as she picked up cups and plates and carried them to the break room.

"Did you see that cute afghan? It's fun to think Joel had been wrapped up in it."

"And probably spit up on it or pooped on it."

That caused Kennedy to laugh as she put her feet on the floor and pushed herself up to stand. "I have never felt so ungraceful in my life," she said as she waddled behind Hillary to the break room.

"But you've never looked so beautiful."

"Neither have you," Kennedy returned the compliment as she pulled out a chair and sat down. "I always thought you were a happy person, but the past few months, well, your glow isn't just a baby."

Hillary turned and leaned against the counter. "I am happy. I have to admit, I didn't think Chase had it in him to commit and to want to settle down and be a father. But I think it's exactly what he wanted, even if he didn't know it."

"I suppose it helps that you smoothed things over between him and his mom."

"I think she was ready to smooth things over. I just was an outside source to help."

"Either way, he's never seemed happier either," Kennedy said as she winced and pressed a hand to her side.

Hillary moved to her. "What was that? What are you doing?"

Kennedy laughed and adjusted in her chair. "Relax. I get them from time to time. I'm not in labor. I have weeks."

"You're in prime any day status."

Kennedy shook her head. "Braxton Hicks contractions. I am not going into labor. This baby is so comfortable, I'm not sure she'll ever come out."

Pulling out the chair next to Kennedy, Hillary sat down. "What's her name?"

The smile on Kennedy's face grew wide and she shook her head. "You'll find out at the hospital when you come to meet her."

"I can't believe you're not going to tell me."

"It's the only surprise I have left. I'm not like you. I couldn't wait to find out."

Hillary rubbed her hands over her belly, just as Kennedy had done earlier. "Truth is, this one won't give up the secret, and I can't see having some big test done to find out. I can't imagine Chase's kid wouldn't want to flaunt whatever is between their legs."

"Hey," his voice came from the doorway as he and Joel walked into the room. "I'll have you know I've never wandered around and flaunted that myself."

Hillary narrowed her eyes on him. "Never?"

"That was for private showings only," he said as he bent to kiss her gently on the lips. "I'll load up your truck. Is it that big pink pile in the middle of the room?"

Kennedy nodded. "Mostly. And thank you."

Joel remained in the room looking between the two women leaned back in their chairs rubbing their bellies.

"I don't think I've ever seen anything so beautiful than the two of you looking so miserable. And I mean that in the sincerest way."

Kennedy took his hand and rested it on her stomach. "She's been dancing at her party all day."

"God, that's going to cost a fortune, isn't it? Dance."

That made Hillary snort when she laughed. "Suddenly I'm praying for a boy."

"You danced when we were younger," Kennedy reminded her.

"I did. My mom worked two jobs to be a dance mom, and it was horrible. Horrible. My feet bled. I'm sure she ripped out more hair than she got into those tight buns in my hair. The girls were mean and snobby."

"I've never heard you say that before."

Hillary shrugged her shoulders. "It wasn't important before. Now I think about this baby and who they'll be, and I'm scared to death. Boy or girl, I think I'd rather them play hockey. They could get some frustration out instead of being catty and backstabbing."

Joel ran his hand over the back of his neck. "You're not making this very appealing."

"Your baby will have Kennedy Devereaux-Kingsley as her mother. It'll be different. You'll be there for her."

And in that moment, Hillary realized it wasn't dance lessons that turned her off such things, it was the key she'd kept to the front door of their house in her pocket since she'd been seven that made her defensive. Her mother worked two jobs until Hillary moved away from home. Chase might have always had a stick up his ass about his father, and what he'd done, but his father had been present. Her father—well—she'd met him exactly four times in thirty-six years. Chances were, if he walked by her on the street, they wouldn't even know each other.

Kennedy's hand rested on hers and she lifted her tear-filled eyes to see the worry in Kennedy's.

"Are you okay? You got really quiet."

Hillary batted away the tears. "I'm fine. I don't think I'll ever get used to being so emotional."

Joel kissed the top of Kennedy's head. "I think Chase is almost done loading everything. Now's my time to go ask how I can help," he humored. Then he turned to Hillary. "Hey, if you need anything, we're always here."

"I appreciate that," she said as he walked out of the room.

The only thing she decided she needed in that moment was to take her mother a bouquet of flowers and thank her for everything she did to make Hillary's life easier—because Hillary felt as if she might have made that job a little harder for her mom.

CHAPTER 42

Since Gladys wasn't open on Sundays, Hillary sent Chase on his way, and stopped at the grocery store for a bouquet of flowers, and a box of chocolate chip cookies from the bakery.

When Hillary was young, and she'd had a bad day, her mom would make cookies and they'd sit at the table and have a heart to heart.

As she drove to her mother's house, guilt rose in Hillary's chest. How many nights had she had her at the kitchen table until midnight or two in the morning just crying over mean girls or stupid boys? Her mother had plenty of other things that she needed to tend to, and yet, she sat there while Hillary cried her eyes out.

Hillary parked her car in front of her mother's house and noticed her mother sitting on the porch, still dressed in the outfit she'd worn to Kennedy's baby shower.

As she stepped out of the car her mother stood and started toward her.

"Did I forget something at the store?" she asked.

Hillary pulled the box of cookies and the bouquet of flowers from the back seat and shut the door. "No. I just thought I'd come by for a visit."

Her mother stopped halfway down the walk and waited for her. "You are glowing, Hill."

"I brought these for you," Hillary said handing her mother the flowers.

"This is sweet. What do you have there?"

"Cookies. Do you have time to sit and eat some?"

Her mother wrapped her arm around Hillary's shoulders. "I always have time, sweetheart."

And she always did, Hillary knew.

They sat down at the same kitchen table her mother had since Hillary was little, overlooking the same small patch of yard, but now it had a thriving garden and no swing set.

Her mother poured them each a glass of milk, and Hillary smiled widely as it was set in front of her. "Almost like old times."

When her mother sat down, she opened the box of cookies. "Why almost?"

"The cookies are probably stale and not warm and fresh baked."

Her mother laughed as she set four cookies on a napkin between them and closed the box. "Well, had I known you were coming..."

"I didn't know I was coming." Hillary reached a hand out and covered her mother's. "I just wanted to come over and say I'm sorry and thank you." Her voice shook at the end and she'd really hoped to get more than a few words out before she broke down like a blubbering idiot.

Her mother handed her a napkin for the tears that had started to roll down her cheeks. "What are you sorry about?"

Hillary wiped at the tears. "For not being easy to raise."

"Oh, sweetheart, when have I ever told you that you weren't easy to raise?"

"Never. It's just now, thinking about my future, my baby's

future, I think of how hard you worked and all that you did to provide for me. And I always took it as neglect or you didn't care, but deep inside, I knew differently. I knew you did what you needed to do to keep us afloat. Hell, I got to do all the things I wanted, but at what cost to you?"

Her mother moved her chair so that they were side by side, and she wrapped her arm around Hillary's shoulders. "Eighteen years, Hill. That's all I got. Eighteen years. Then you were off on your own adventure, paying your own way, doing your own things. Then I could do my own and watch you thrive because I'd done my best. In the scheme of things, it was such a short time. And it was all my honor to get to work so hard to give you the best life. No, it wasn't easy, and I had a lot of sleepless nights. But I knew someday, you would understand everything. I'm just sorry it was only the two of us."

"I'm not. I'd rather have only had you than to have had someone here who didn't want to be."

"You were and are my world. And I can't wait to spoil this baby," her mother said as she rested a hand on Hillary's stomach. "And for the record. I have always had a soft spot for Chase Devereaux, even if I always thought he was trouble." She laughed and Hillary pressed her forehead to her mother's.

"He is trouble."

"But he loves you so much. And I know you've always had feelings for him. As far back as I can remember."

"I thought they were brotherly feelings. I guess I was wrong about that."

"And aren't you glad?"

"So very glad."

HILLARY'S VISIT with her mother had done her heart good. Maybe there was a new understanding between two mothers, and not

just a child and her mother. There certainly was a new appreciation on Hillary's behalf.

On her way home, she stopped by the store and picked up
groceries for dinner. She wanted to spoil her husband tonight.
She didn't have many meals she was an expert at making, but her
mother had taught her to make an amazing meatloaf, and she was
going to wow Chase with it, or she hoped she would.

When she pulled up to the house Chase and Max were
standing outside looking at the house. Max had an iPad in his
hand. What were they up to, she wondered?

They both walked toward her car as she parked, turned off
the engine, and stepped out.

"What are you two up to?"

"Making plans." Chase leaned in and kissed her softly. "Did
you get groceries?"

"Yes."

"We'll carry them inside for you," he offered, and she watched
his brother tuck the iPad behind his back in the waistband of his
pants.

Hillary followed them into the house. "What kinds of plans
are you discussing?"

Max set the bags he'd carried in on the counter and pulled out
the iPad. "Just a few improvements and future additions. For
down the line."

Hillary looked at the iPad. "You just drew this up?"

"It's what I do."

"And you do amazing work. The work you did at the shop
makes Kennedy's office so much roomier."

"That was the point."

Hillary zoomed into the screen. "Is this a master bathroom
added to the master bedroom?"

Chase moved in behind her and wrapped his arms around
her, resting his hands on her belly. "You deserve it. And there's
plans for another bedroom down the line," he offered.

"Why don't we just move?"

"Because we can afford this house, pay it off, and live nicely. Then we can travel and take our kids to Disney whenever we want to."

She eased her head back to rest on his shoulder. "Your finance brain at work again?"

"It's seated deeply."

Max tucked the iPad under his arm. "You two are making me sick. I think I'll make my exit."

Chase laughed and slapped his brother on the back. "You're just jealous."

"Maybe I'm lucky," Max retorted. "I dodged the bullet."

"I wish I could believe you."

Hillary moved to the counter and began to pull items from the bags. "Do you really feel like that, Max? I mean, Meghann moved because she had the opportunity of a lifetime. It's not like she broke your heart with bad intentions."

She saw Max's jaw set.

"She did what she needed to do. I'm here building my business. She's in New York living her dream. We'd have both been miserable had we followed the other. But it's how I feel. If we'd have been married, one of us would hate the other for what they'd missed out on."

Her heart broke for him, but perhaps he was right. They'd given up their prefect relationship, and she and Chase had taken their sweet time to dive into theirs. The world would be a nicer place if everyone could be happy, she thought. But Max was a good guy. No doubt happiness was on the horizon for him too.

CHAPTER 43

Seotember gave way to October, and the two very pregnant women at *Kennedy Devereaux Designs*, waddled through the store as Paige unpacked boxes and restocked the inventory.

"You know, I have half a mind to go get pregnant and make you both teach my yoga classes, and I'm just going to sit and watch you do it," she said as she placed a new handbag on the shelf.

Kennedy rubbed her belly, her bare feet propped up on a chair. "Do it. I dare you," she said to her sister who rolled her eyes.

Hillary paced a small circle rubbing her back. The baby had been moving around a lot, and she hadn't gotten any sleep the night before, and now she was incredibly uncomfortable.

"You doing okay?" Kennedy asked.

"I'm uncomfortable. Not as uncomfortable as you look though," she commented.

"I've heard that first babies take longer. I was kind of hoping she'd give me a little bit of a break. She's due in four days, and seriously, I don't think she's in any hurry."

Hillary stopped pacing and pressed her hand to her side as a pain ripped through her.

Paige moved to her. "Are you okay?"

"I'm fine. I'm fine," she repeated as she blew a breath out trying to ease the pain that lingered, but another one started.

"You need to sit down."

"I can't move," she said gripping Paige's arm. "It'll go away in a moment." Hillary continued to blow out breaths trying to calm herself and her baby down.

Kennedy managed to her feet and moved to them. "Something's wrong. You shouldn't be having labor pains like that yet. I haven't even had any."

Paige shot her sister a look, her eyes narrowed. "Just because you got knocked up first doesn't mean Hillary isn't going to have her baby first."

Both Hillary and Kennedy exchanged wide eyed looks.

"I'm going to what?" Hillary shot out the question as another pain ripped through her.

"I didn't mean to be insensitive," Kennedy said with tears filling her eyes.

Paige shook her head. "Oh, would the two of you stop it. We need to get Hillary to the hospital. That's all I'm trying to say."

"Call Chase," Hillary bit out the words as another pain caused her to lean forward and take hold of Paige's shoulders. "Get him here."

"I'll call him," Kennedy promised.

Paige wrapped an arm around Hillary's waist and guided her to the back of the store so they could walk out the back door and out to Paige's car.

When they got outside, Joel hurried toward them from the back door of the tap house.

"Is she okay?" he asked running toward them and moving in on Hillary's other side, his arm around her waist.

"I think she's in labor. We need to get her to the hospital. She's having contractions one on top the other."

"Where is Chase?"

Hillary let out a growl as another pain caught her breath. "Driving to the airport. He had a client to pick up."

Paige opened the door to her car. "Kennedy is calling him now."

They eased Hillary into the passenger seat. "I'll follow up on that and we'll get him there even if I have to pick up his client."

Hillary reached for his hand. "Thank you."

CHASE HAD RECEIVED Kennedy's call just as he'd pulled up to his client's house and was helping them to the car. In his frantic state, the client had encouraged him to leave them and hurry to the hospital. They would catch a cab; his baby was more important.

In all of the excitement he'd kissed the wife of his client on the cheek.

Now, at the hospital, he didn't even know where to go. Paige had texted him that they were going in through the emergency room, so he headed that way.

Chase pushed through the door and to the front counter. "I'm looking for my wife. She's having a baby." he said, his voice rising in pitch and volume.

The woman behind the counter looked up at him, as did the nurse who had been talking to her.

"Chase?" The nurse said his name and pulled her mask from her face.

"Tammi."

His stomach twisted as he saw her standing there. He hadn't seen her since he'd left her at the doorway to the chapel in her wedding dress.

Tammi pushed her shoulders back. "You're looking for your wife?"

Chase swallowed hard. "Yes."

"Hillary?"

"Yes," he said, noticing her eyes had gone moist.

"I was right, huh? She was pregnant?" He heard the wavering in her voice. "You decided to marry her, huh?"

Running his hand over his hair he moved closer to the counter, the woman seated at the desk looking between them.

"The baby is my baby—our baby."

Tammi batted her eyes, as if to force the tears away. "Oh. I didn't expect that."

"I hadn't either."

"Well, congratulations."

"Thank you." He looked at the woman who was watching them. "Is she here? Hillary Devereaux?"

The woman looked at the screen. "They just moved her up to labor and delivery."

Chase felt the blood drain from his face. "Delivery? She still has weeks to go."

"Babies come when they're ready. Delivery is on the third floor. You just go to the elevators and..."

Tammi rested a hand on the woman's shoulder. "I'll take him."

Though he didn't like the idea of spending even a moment with her, he graciously accepted her guidance and followed her to the elevator.

Once it arrived, they stepped in. "I'm happy for you, Chase. I really am."

"Tammi, I'm so sorry. I couldn't have imagined something like this..."

She held up her hand. "There was always something there. I knew that the moment I met her. And deep inside, I knew she would be the reason you and I wouldn't work out. I thought being married would be an adventure, but it looks like you got the adventure. I knew you loved her, Chase. I just thought you loved me more."

No, he knew he'd never loved her as he loved Hillary. No one had ever, nor would ever get that distinction.

When the elevator opened, they both stepped out. "The nurses' station is at the end of the hallway. And, Chase, I am happy for you. Congratulations on your marriage and your baby. I hope you have a happy life. I really do."

The urgency to get to Hillary was a strong pull, but he needed to close this part of his life.

Chase moved to Tammi and hugged her, pressing a kiss to her cheek. "Thank you."

He felt the trail of tears against his lips as he moved away and hurried down the hall toward his wife and his baby

P aige was pacing the hallway when he spotted her. The moment she saw him, she hurried to him.

"You're here," she nearly pulled him to her weeping. "You need to get to her."

"Paige, what's wrong? Hillary? She's okay? The baby?"

Paige sucked in a breath. "Something happened. Something is wrong. They won't let me in, but they'll let you in. I don't know any more than that."

Chase's head began to swim, and again he could feel the blood drain from it, but he couldn't move. He clung to Paige like a lifeline.

"Go. You need to get to her."

She moved to the door and pushed it open. All Chase could see were monitors, doctors, and nurses moving around Hillary. He stepped into the room, and eyes moved to him.

"Chase!" Hillary cried out as they worked to add sensors to her skin.

He moved to her and took her hand as the doctor moved the ultrasound wand over her stomach. "What's going on? You're not due for four weeks. What happened?"

Hillary gripped his hand and let out a scream.

"Your wife has gone into labor, but the baby is in distress. She's turned her position and is now breech. We're monitoring the baby's heart and then we're going to move your wife into surgery."

Chase leaned against the side of the bed, Hillary still gripping tightly to his hand. "Surgery?"

"We're going to have to take the baby caesarian. We have to get to her quickly."

"You keep saying her. Hillary?"

The doctor smiled. "Your daughter. She's in distress and that is causing distress to your wife. We need to get them into surgery."

Chase looked down at Hillary whose face had turned bright red. "A girl? We're having a girl?"

"Chase, don't let anything happen to her," Hillary cried. "You stay with her. You go with her when she's born. And you take care of her if something happens to me."

He hadn't even considered something like that could be possible. "Nothing is going to happen, Hill. You're going to be fine." He pressed a kiss to the top of her head. "You're going to be okay, sweetheart. You're going to come out of there just fine."

"Call my mom."

"I will."

The doctor looked toward them both. "We're going to take her now and get her prepped. A nurse will help you gown up and we'll see you in there."

Hillary held on to his hand until they got to the door. Chase stood and watched until they had gone through another door and disappeared.

A nurse pulled Chase down the hall to another room. She helped him gown up.

"I'm going in there?" Chase asked the nurse.

"Yes. They're prepping her now."

Chase pulled the cap over his hair. "Is my wife in danger?"

"This is routine. She's going to be taken care of."

"But is she in danger?"

The nurse's eyes widened and then went soft. "There is some danger, but like I said, it's routine. The doctors are going to take good care of both of them."

Once Chase was ready, the nurse escorted him into the delivery room. Hillary was on the table, and a drape shielded her from seeing her exposed belly.

Chase could feel his knees go weak, and the nurse must have been trained to notice that. She pulled a chair over next to Hillary's head and eased him into it.

"You'll be fine right here," she said.

Chase looked at Hillary, whose bottom lip trembled. "Are you okay?"

She looked up at him. "I'm scared. Something is wrong, Chase. Something is wrong."

Chase took her hand. "They're going to take care of you. Just breath in and out."

"The baby?"

He didn't have any answers. "She'll be okay," he promised with a sinking heart. "You just keep your mind clear."

Chase sat on his chair, holding his wife's hand, as one nurse sat by her side monitoring her. Doctors and other nurses were shielded behind the drape.

Monitors beeped, and doctors spoke in hushed tones, but Chase could only hear his own heartbeat in his ears. There was a confusion in his heart. Was he supposed to be joyous or fearful? His own legs wouldn't even hold him up. How was it possible that in moments he and Hillary were going to be parents?

Then he heard the doctors talking faster. Was something wrong? Were they going to walk out of that hospital without a baby?

The very thought had his body trembling and tears rolling

down his cheeks.

Hillary squeezed his hand. "What's wrong? Something's wrong."

Chase wiped away the tears as a nurse moved to Hillary's side. "She's tangled herself in the umbilical cord. She has it wrapped around herself and her neck."

The room spun again, but Chase wasn't going let go of his senses. "What now?" he managed.

"They're easing her out and we're going to work on her."

The doctor's voice rose above the others' and Chase knew his daughter was in his hands, but he couldn't look around the drape. His heart couldn't take it.

The nurse that had been next to Hillary hurried to the other side of the room.

"What's happening?" Hillary asked, and he noted the tears that ran down her cheeks.

"I don't know. I don't know, sweetheart," he repeated.

He caught sight of the nurse swiftly moving the baby to the warmer, her skin purple, and she wasn't crying. Wasn't she supposed to be crying?

The tears rolled down his cheeks harder. Had they lost her?

The nurse that had spoken to them earlier came back toward them. "We're going to take her into the NICU. The cord was around her neck, and it had cut off the oxygen supply to the brain. The doctor was able to get her out of the situation. They're going to get her oxygen and her vitals situated." The nurse shifted her eyes to Chase. "Do you want to go with her?"

He exchanged looks with Hillary. How could he leave her laying there like this?

Hillary squeezed his hand again. "Go. Go with her. Don't let her out of your sight."

Chase leaned in and pressed a kiss to her damp forehead. "I love you."

"I love you. Go. Go take care of her."

CHAPTER 45

Hillary drifted in and out of sleep in the sterile room, or was she in the same room? Her eyelids were heavy, and her nose itched from the drugs they'd given her.

She lifted her arm, which was still connected to tubes and wires.

"What can I do for you, sweetie?" her mother's voice came through the darkness.

"Mom?" Her voice was weak and unrecognizable to even herself.

"Yes." She saw her come into view as her mother walked to the side of her bed. "I'm glad to see you awake. You've been in and out for hours."

"Hours?"

Her mother took her hand. "Chase will be back in here in a moment. He was feeding the baby."

"She's alive? She's okay?"

Her mother let out a tiny laugh, but even in the dimly lit room, Hillary could hear the tears. "She's going to be just fine," she said as the door opened, and Hillary saw her husband standing there. "I'll let you two have some time."

Her mother kissed her forehead, and then kissed Chase on the cheek before she left.

Chase took the spot her mother had been standing, and he leaned down to kiss her ever so gently.

"I'm glad to see you awake," his voice shook as he spoke.

"Why was I asleep? I should have just been taken into recovery, right?"

Chase pulled a chair over to the side of her bed and sat down. With her hand in his, he kissed her fingers. "After they took the baby, and I left with her, you began to hemorrhage. They had to give you a hysterectomy to stop it."

"A hysterectomy?"

He nodded. "Hill, you're here. Our baby is here. You're going to be okay, and she's okay too."

Hillary batted away the tears that filled her eyes. "She's okay?"

He nodded and pressed kisses to her fingers again. "They stabilized her and got her to breathe. She was under an oxygen bubble for a few hours, now she's just on oxygen. Just for a little while. The nurses in there are amazing and they're taking good care of her. She was already six pounds." He chuckled. "And she's so beautiful."

"I want to see her."

"They said as soon as you were awake and stable too."

Hillary wiped at the tears that fell. "But I can't have any more children."

Chase wiped at his eyes too. "There are millions of children who need us, if we decide we need more. Hillary, all that matters right now is that our princess is healthy and with us." He lifted his hand to her cheek and gazed into her eyes. "I didn't know I wanted this so much, Hill. She's so perfect."

"We have to name her."

"We didn't discuss it, so I didn't give her a name. But I think she looks just like you. She's beautiful, but her hair is redder."

"Redder?" Hillary laughed. "My mom had red hair when she was little."

"Well, then we know where she gets it."

The door opened again, and a nurse entered. "You're looking better."

"I want to see my daughter."

The nurse moved to the other side of the bed and looked at the monitors and IV. "Let me get some readings and check your sutures. Then maybe we can get you into a chair and you can meet your baby. She's beautiful."

CHASE WATCHED the nurse examine his wife and keep her calm, but he wasn't calm inside.

He'd thought his childhood was traumatizing, and the mistakes of his parents had branded him for life, but nothing would erase the moment he thought he might lose the two women he loved most in the world.

Biting down on his lip, hard, he forced himself to smile at Hillary, who was chatting with the nurse as if she were feeling herself. Just a few feet down the hall, their baby was being cared for by some of the sweetest women he'd ever met.

It was all okay, but the moment he was alone at home, or in a bathroom, he was going to lose it. He knew it. But not now. Not in front of Hillary.

THE NURSE HELPED Hillary into a wheelchair, and Chase pushed her toward the NICU. He walked her through the protocol at the door of washing and sanitizing before they went in to see their daughter.

There was a giddiness that filled her belly and pushed away the physical pain and the emotional pain of knowing she'd only ever give birth to one baby.

Chase didn't have to tell her they were coming up to her room. She could feel her. As he pushed her through the enlarged doorway, she saw her baby and began to cry.

"Hey," Chase moved to her. "Why the tears?"

"Happy tears. I swear they're happy."

The NICU nurse assigned to their baby moved in beside her and introduced herself and gave her all the details on what their princess had been through in her short few hours. "She'll stay here for a bit until she's able to go home with you. She's still considered premature, having given you a four week jump start," she said smiling. "We're going to take care of her and you need to let us. You need to recover too, so that when she does come home, you'll both be ready for each other."

Hillary wiped away the tears. "Okay."

"Are you going to nurse her?"

"I'd like to try."

"Let's get her latched to you. Do you have a name for this little one?"

Chase and Hillary exchanged looks. She reached for his hand. "We never discussed it. How is it we never had this talk?"

Chase chuckled. "We've had a crazy year, so far. We sidelined this to deal with all of it."

"I guess you're right." She watched as the nurse lifted her daughter from the bassinette and collected the cords that were still attached to her.

The moment she saw her, the tears were back. She never knew she could feel so much love for someone as she did at that moment when the nurse laid her in her arms.

"She's all pink. With her red hair, the blush of her skin, her tiny little fingernails, and her rosebud lips." Hillary looked up at Chase. "Her name is Kennedy."

Chase laughed. "Oh, that's going to give my sister a big head. But, okay." He reached for her little hand. Hello, Miss Kennedy."

The nurse helped Hillary latch Kennedy to her, and though she didn't take to it right away, they kept at it.

Chase checked his phone when it buzzed. "Her namesake is here," he laughed looking up at the nurse. "Will they be able to come and visit?"

She smiled. "One at a time."

Chase kissed Hillary on the top of the head. "I'll go get her first. Let's let her make a big deal out of it before everyone else gets to us."

Hillary nodded as she watched her tiny daughter suckle at her breast.

CHAPTER 46

Chase walked out to the waiting room where his sisters, his brother, and Joel waited. His mother, and his mother-in-law looked up at him from mid-conversation.

"We have a little girl," he said as Paige rushed him and flung her arms around him.

"You're a girl daddy," she said planting a noisy kiss on his cheek. "God, you're out of your element."

Kennedy waddled to him and hugged him. "I can't wait to meet her."

"Well, you're first. Hillary would like you to go back. I'll take you in, we can only have one at a time. She's in the NICU, we had some complications, but everyone is okay now."

"I can't believe you're a father before I'm a mother."

"You are a mother. You just haven't met your princess yet."

He took his sister's hand and walked her through the doors to the NICU and the process he'd taken Hillary through.

Hillary was sitting with their daughter pressed to her bare skin when they walked in.

"Hey, Hill. How are you?" Kennedy's voice was soft.

Hillary looked up at Chase and then back at Kennedy. "I'm good. We're both good."

"I'll leave you two alone," Chase said, dipping his head down to kiss his wife and his daughter, then kissing his sister's head.

HILLARY BRUSHED her hand gently over her daughter's soft red hair as Kennedy took the seat next to her.

"Hillary, she's beautiful," Kennedy said through her tears. "God, she's perfect. And she's all pink."

"That's what I told Chase when I named her." She shifted her gaze to the woman who had been a sister to her for as long as she could remember. "I told him that her hair was pink, her skin was pink, and her nails were pink. Her name is Kennedy."

Kennedy raised her fingers to her trembling lips. "Kennedy?"

Hillary nodded. "It seemed appropriate. You're my best friend, a sister I didn't have, and the reason I have the love of my life with me. Without you, I wouldn't have this."

Kennedy rose slowly from her chair and wrapped an arm around Hillary, looking down at the baby. "I'm so honored I could burst."

"I love you, Kennedy. She'll be my only child, and I can't think of anyone better to name her after."

Kennedy sat back down. "Oh, I don't think you'll keep him away from you and only have one."

Hillary batted the tears from her eyes. "We had some complications."

"Chase said that."

"She turned breech and they had to take her c-section. Her cord was wrapped around her neck and she didn't have any oxygen."

Kennedy's fingers pressed to her lips again. "Oh, Hill."

"Well, I hemorrhaged, and they had to give me a hysterectomy."

"Your mom said you'd tell me all about it. She wouldn't tell me anything."

"I can't have any more children."

"There are millions of children..."

"I know. That's what Chase said. But none of them will look like him."

"You're happy?"

"I'm deliriously happy. I never thought this was in the cards for me. Would you like to hold her?"

Kennedy nodded and moved in to gather the cords and the blanket that wrapped around the baby. She held her to her chest and the tears flowed down her cheeks.

"I love her."

Hillary laughed. "They'll get to grow up together, just like we did."

"They'll be best friends," Kennedy said and then her eyes went wide. "Oh, no."

"What's wrong?"

She held the baby back out to Hillary and pressed her hands to her stomach. "My water just broke."

Two hours later, Chase pushed the wheelchair with his wife into the room where Kennedy held her daughter in her arms. Everyone was welcome together, unlike in the NICU, and he wondered if it was going to make Hillary sad. She was smiling, but deep down did the differences in the births of their daughters matter?

Kennedy's mother moved to Chase and hugged him, then bent to hug Hillary. "Congratulations on your new baby too. Kennedy told me her name. It's one of the best names out there," she said.

"Thank you." Hillary looked past her to Kennedy whose baby was twice the size of theirs. "What's her name?"

"Matilda Mary-June Kingsley," she boasted. "Her middle name is for her grandmothers. We'll call her Mati."

Chase smiled when he saw both of their mothers grinning, since their names had been combined as a middle name. They hadn't considered Kennedy's middle name yet.

Joel moved to Chase and put his arm around his shoulders. "This has to be the craziest week of our lives, huh?"

"I thought I was prepared, but I'm not," Chase admitted.

"I think we'll make it. Now it's Paige's and Max's turn."

Paige rolled her eyes, but Max's narrowed his. Chase gave him a brotherly nod, but he knew the discussion of babies, and the marriages that had happened that year had taken their toll on him. He'd been the one ready to get married and have kids, but it hadn't worked out that way. Now he was an observer, and it had to sting.

But Max's eyes had lit up when Kennedy handed her baby to him and he held her like a skilled uncle would.

Hillary reached up and took Chase's hand. "I think I need to go back to my room and rest," she said softly.

"Okay."

"Kennedy, she's beautiful. I can't wait until we're all freed from this place and can spend time together."

"Soon, Hill. It'll be real soon."

Chase pushed Hillary down the hall and back to her room. He helped her into bed before a nurse walked in to check on her and her incisions.

"I'm going to go home and get us some clothes. I'll be back in an hour," he said.

"You should stay home and get some rest. You're so tired."

Chase shook his head. "I'm never going to leave your side. I'll sleep here tonight and every night until you're home with me. And I'll be right next to you when she's home with us too. I'll get up to help you feed her, and I'll do my part, Hill. I didn't know this was what I wanted more than anything, but I'm so damned happy I could burst."

"Even if she's our only one?"

"Hillary, I was this happy before she came along. It's having you as my wife that fulfills me. Having little Kennedy, well, that's the biggest bonus anyone could have ever given me."

"I love you," Hillary said as she blinked heavy lids.

"I love you. Get some sleep, and I'll be back."

EPILOGUE

Kennedy's pink store was decorated for Christmas, and it made the store sparkle even more.

Hillary and Kennedy sat in the expanded office, each of them in a rocking chair, nursing their daughters. The small TV Max had mounted on the wall had on a cooking show that neither of them were paying attention to.

Paige poked her head around the corner. "Do we have any more little white boxes for designer jewelry? I'm about to sell the last two bracelets you have out here."

"In the cabinet in the break room."

Paige nodded and darted back out.

Hillary moved her daughter from her breast to her shoulder. "I guess you'll need to spend our week off before New Year's designing some new pieces."

"Joel designed me some new shelves, drawers, and little boxes like he used to make his mother, to organize my tools and beads. I do feel the need to get creative again."

Their attention was drawn to the TV again as the next cooking show began.

"I'm happy for her," Kennedy said, looking at the blonde on

the TV who smiled wide, as if she were smiling at the two new moms watching her. "She's living her dream."

Meghann Carr began chopping fresh vegetables on a board, and Hillary wondered if Kennedy even noticed the bracelet on Meghann's arm. It had been one of Kennedy's first pieces.

"I guess Max could watch her every day, right?" Hillary asked as her daughter fell asleep and she eased her into the bassinet in the office.

"He probably doesn't even have a TV, just so he doesn't accidentally see her face."

Hillary buttoned up her top and straightened her skirt. "I'm going to go help Paige."

She walked out to the showroom with its white trees, pink ornaments, and twinkling lights just as Chase walked through the front door.

She would never tire of seeing him smile at her when he saw her, only now, she could move in and kiss him any time she wanted.

"Do you have a few minutes?" he asked, taking her hand.

Hillary exchanged glances with Paige, who nodded. "I guess I do."

He escorted her out of the store, and hand in hand they walked down the street. "Are we going much further? Kennedy's asleep in the nursery."

"She'll be fine for a moment." They turned the corner to the next block and the small office building at the end of the street. "There."

She looked at the building that housed six small offices.

"There what?"

"Look at the sign."

Devereaux Limo was the newest name on the sign.

"What does that mean?"

"It means I have an actual office to work from. I just picked up a new client that contracted with me to be their exclusive service. I'll be able to add one more car to my fleet."

Hillary turned to him. "Can we afford that?"

"We can. And it's got two offices, so Max is going to help me fix it up so Kennedy can spend time with me too."

Hillary rested her head on his shoulder. "In your office?"

"Yes. I told you, I'm all in on this. When Joel has Mati, I'll have Kennedy. Then you and Kennedy can focus on the store."

"I never pictured you as a perfect girl dad."

"Or a dad at all."

"Well, there is that. So you're going to be down the street doing book work?"

Chase chuckled as he wrapped his arm around her shoulders. "Actually I hired a woman to do that."

"Oh," Hillary swallowed hard. "A woman?"

"Yeah, she claims to be the baby's grandmother, but I don't trust her." He smiled.

"You hired your mother?"

"I did. And if my father comes back in town, he'll have a place in my organization too. I've spent too much time putting blame on them and not enjoying the opportunity they gave me."

"What was that?"

"To be me. To excel where I wanted to, and to be the perfect husband and father. They did the best they could do. I have to give them credit for that. Our story didn't play out like the perfect fairytale either."

"It's perfect now," she reminded him.

"Absolutely perfect."

ABOUT THE AUTHOR

Bestselling Author Bernadette Marie is known for building families readers want to be part of. Her series The Keller Family has graced bestseller charts since its release in 2011. Since then she has authored and published over forty books. The married mother of five sons promises romances with a *Happily Ever After always*...and says she can write it because she lives it.

Obsessed with the art of writing and the business of publishing, chronic entrepreneur Bernadette Marie established her own publishing house, 5 Prince Publishing, in 2011 to bring her own work to market as well as offer an opportunity for fresh voices in fiction to find a home as well. Bernadette is also an educator in the industry, offering workshops and speaking at conferences. In 2020 she was named the Independent Writer of the Year from the Rocky Mountain Fiction Writers.

When not immersed in the writing/publishing world, Bernadette Marie and her husband are shuffling their five hockey playing boys around town to practices and games as well as running their family business. She is a lover of a good stout craft beer and might be slightly addicted to chocolate.

We hope you enjoyed book two in the Devereaux Family Series, *Chase Devereaux*. Please enjoy an excerpt from book three, *Max Devereaux*.

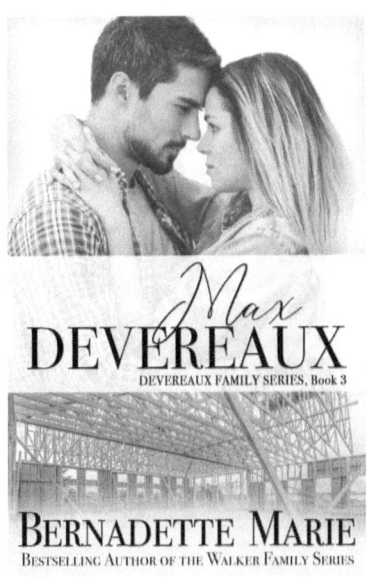

MAX DEVEREAUX

The orange Home Depot bucket full of tools was balanced on the tailgate of Max's Ford F-150. He fastened his tool belt, and then took a sip of coffee from his travel mug.

His morning ritual had always been a hot cup of coffee he brewed himself, country music on his radio, and the sunrise out his window as he drove his construction sites and checked on their progress. He was still finishing a remodel on his brother's house, and he'd be done with that within the week.

His brother and sister-in-law had wanted a master bathroom added to the house, as well as a little more space, now that they had their baby. Max's niece was almost six months old, and the house was looking amazing, he thought.

Lifting the bucket and lowering it to the ground, Max pushed up the tailgate and locked it. He'd had enough tools stolen over the years, it was worth the thirty seconds to lock everything up tight each time.

As he turned to walk up toward the house, a car pulled up behind him, so he stopped. It was then he noticed the New York plates on the car. The hand holding his cup of coffee began to tremble, and the bucket started to slip from his grasp..

Instead of dropping the tools to the ground, he set the bucket down and waited for the driver to step out of the car.

The moment he saw her, his tongue swelled in his mouth and his heart rate kicked up to an uncomfortable pace.

"Good morning, Max," her voice was soft and gentle, just like she was.

"Meghann," he said, surprised he could even get that out. "What are you doing here?"

She stayed safely behind her car door. "I hope you don't mind. Paige told me where to find you. I took her yoga class this morning." As she moved away from the car he noticed the outfit she wore. Yoga pants and some fitted top that hugged her beautiful body.

"What are you doing back here? Aren't you still filming your show?"

"It's on break," she said inching toward him. "Listen, I was hoping to talk to you about a job."

Max took another sip of his coffee, nearly choking on its bitter taste. "What kind of job?"

"My brother and I want to have some work done on our mom's house. She's recently been diagnosed with Alzheimers and her house needs updating and some safety features added."

Max took a step toward her and reached for her hand. "I'm so sorry to hear about your mom. I should have kept in touch with her."

"That's why we came looking for you. She always loved you, so she'd be comfortable with you in her house."

"How soon are you looking at starting this?"

"As soon as you can. She's walking with a walker, and her bathroom has to be fitted. The kitchen is old and..."

He gave her hand a squeeze. "You can walk me through it later. Of course I'll do that for you."

He noticed the curtains in the front window moving, and he assumed that they were being watched.

Meghann must have noticed too. "I should let you go. I think your client is waiting for you."

Still holding her hand, he gazed into dark eyes that he'd missed. "Would you like to see those clients? They have someone special in there."

"Whose house is this?"

"Chase and Hillary's."

Her eyes went wide. "Chase and Hillary are married?"

He chuckled. That was a common reaction to his brother marrying his sister's best friend. "Not only are they married; they have a baby."

Meghann raised her other hand to her heart. "I can't even believe it."

Neither could he. "Would you like to say hello?"

"I would."

Max let go of her hand and picked up his bucket. They headed toward the front door as it opened. Hillary stepped out with his niece Kennedy on her hip.

"Oh, look who is town," she squealed as she reached out an arm to hug Meghann and Kennedy took a handful of her hair. "I'm sorry," Hillary said, taking her daughter's hand and releasing the hair.

"I can't believe you and Chase have a baby."

Hillary kissed her daughter on the head. "Neither can I. More surprising is that he's an amazing and attentive father."

Max nodded. "I have to agree. Who would have thought Chase had it in him?"

Meghann laughed. "I should let Max get to work."

Hillary shook her head. "Do you have time for a cup of coffee? I'd love to catch up."

"Can I take a raincheck? I need to get back to my mom. I'll be in town for the week at least. I'd love to see everyone."

Max bit down on the inside of his cheek. One week. His heart was going to ache that entire time, but she needed him and he'd be there for her.

"Your number is still the same?" he asked as she turned to walk back toward her car.

Meghann stopped and looked up at him. "Yes."

"I'll call you and make plans to come look at the house."

"I really appreciate that."

Max watched her walk back to her car and drive away.

"Are you going to be able to function?" Hillary asked, and he shifted his attention back to her as he stepped through the front door.

"I'm fine."

"You didn't know she was in town, did you?"

"I did not. Seems as if Paige did."

"She mentioned it."

Max walked toward the bathroom he'd been working on. "No one thought to mention it to me?"

Hillary followed him. "You get a little worked up over her."

"Exactly why I think it would be nice to know she might drive up on me."

"It's not all bad, is it?"

Max set his bucket on the floor. "No, it's never bad. We parted on good terms. I'd have been miserable in New York, and she wouldn't have what she has, had she stayed. We're not compatible, but we can be friendly."

"What did she want to talk to you about?"

Max leaned up against the doorjamb. "Her mother's got Alzheimers."

"Oh, that sucks."

"Ya. Well they want to do some remodeling on her house to help her out."

"And they want you to do it?"

He chuckled. "She would be comfortable with me in the house."

Hillary hitched Kennedy up on her hip. "She trusts you, Max. She knows you'll always be there for her."

And didn't he know it? It's what made getting over her so damn hard.

Other Titles from 5 Prince Publishing
www.5princebooks.com